STACKS

FIRE DANCE

AT

SPIDER ROCK

PRESENTED TO THE

NEWARK PUBLIC LIBRARY

by

Heath
Moundbuilders
Lions Club

FIRE DANCE AT SPIDER ROCK

Les Savage, Jr.

Thorndike Press • Chivers Press
Thorndike, Maine USA   Bath, Avon, England

This Large Print edition is published by Thorndike Press, USA and by Chivers Press, England.

Published in 1996 in the U.S. by arrangement with Golden West Literary Agency.

Published in 1996 in the U.K. by arrangement with Golden West Literary Agency.

U.S Hardcover 0-7862-0805-8 (Western Series Edition)
U.K. Hardcover 0-7451-4978-2 (Chivers Large Print)
U.K. Softcover   0-7451-4979-0 (Camden Large Print)

An earlier version of this novel appeared in condensed magazine form. When the author sought to publish the full-length version, he was compelled to delete many scenes and characters because of editorial conventions in Western fiction book publishing in the early 1950's. *FIRE DANCE AT SPIDER ROCK* has been restored to what the author intended.

Thorndike Large Print® Western Series.

The text of this Large Print edition is unabridged.
Other aspects of the book may vary from the original edition.

Set in 16 pt. Century Schoolbook by Al Chase.

Printed in the United States on permanent paper.

British Library Cataloguing in Publishing Data available

Library of Congress Cataloging in Publication Data

Savage, Les.
  Fire dance at Spider Rock /
  Les Savage, Jr. — Large print ed.
    p.   cm.
  ISBN 0-7862-0805-8 (lg. print : hc)
    1. Large type print. 2. Navajo Indians — Fiction. I. Title.
  [PS3569.A826F57   1996]
  813'.54—dc20   95-33141

FIRE DANCE
AT
SPIDER ROCK

Foreword

T.V. Olsen

I've been writing Western novels for quite a spell. For over forty years, if you count the early never-published ones. Perusing the already-established popular Western novelists of that time — the late 1940s and early 1950s — I found three writers in particular grabbed my interest ahead of any others: Luke Short, Elmore Leonard, and Les Savage, Jr.

Short was the first one I read. I was entranced by his plotlines, his style, his detailed true-to-life descriptions, and the excellence of his characters' dialogue. So I modeled (or tried to model) my first Western attempts after his work. The results were far less than satisfactory because (against my own intentions) I kept diluting my writing with other, largely unconscious, influences. I soon learned it was better to hit my own stride, develop my own approaches and styling, rather than imitate others. But those early nuances remain part of my professional legacy, and toward them I feel everlastingly indebted.

An important influence, beyond any cavil, was Les Savage, Jr. I first came on a condensed magazine version of his novel "The Hide Rustlers" (now restored as COPPER BLUFFS). From that time on, I tried to secure copies of all his books that I could, in the suddenly booming Western paperback market — both originals and reprints of hard cover novels.

No other author in any genre could tell a story in anything like Savage's inimitable way. As with most highly individualistic writers, his technique on one level is difficult to break down and analyze because of its very uniqueness. On another level, its components are easy to single out and isolate for the same reason!

Savage's plots are extremely elaborate, well constructed, carefully knit. His descriptions are very detailed and striking. Reading a Savage novel, you could see in your mind's eyes events unfolding as vividly as if you were watching a motion picture.

All writers of fiction, if they're worth their salt, try to ground themselves thoroughly in the eras and settings in which they're working. But Savage went to painstaking depths of extensive research far beyond any other popular writers of whom I'm aware.

The present book, *FIRE DANCE AT SPIDER ROCK*, is a good example. It takes place on a month-by-month basis in 1862 and deals with a Civil War story set against an intensely localized region in the Tucson, Arizona, area. As in all of Savage's works, the terrain and vegetation are defined with a graphic and atmospheric detail. Yet, very much in the popular Western tradition, the tale is spiced with plenty of fast-moving action . . . and then some!

The Italian director Sergio Leone has been credited with injecting dust-and-grit reality and a blood-and-guts depiction of violence back into recent Western movies (beginning with his spaghetti oaters of the 1960s that made Clint Eastwood a superstar almost overnight). Yet they seem pallid in comparison to Les Savage's treatment of the same in the early 1950s. Some of it is sanguinary enough to curdle the digestion even of a reader of the 1990s.

In the present book I refer you to the lengthy scene in Chapter Three where Yaki Peters subdues a team of fractious mules. It's packed with an extraordinary amount of ferocious vinegar laced with folk humor couched in a raging period vernacular (as Yaki hurls imprecations at the mules) that was one of Savage's trademarks. He could develop pure out-and-out violence to an incredibly savage (pun intended) brutality that's apparent in the saloon brawl described in Chapter Six. For an instance of his ability to describe the taut and gut-freezing suspense of a heavily loaded freight wagon hitched to a team of berserk mules and hurtling down the switchbacks of a precarious mountain trail, see Chapter Seven.

Savage's imagery is an extravagant delight, especially his use of simile. I cite the following: "He thought he caught soft tinkling (spurs], like the jangle of bracelets on a woman's wrist" — or "a face seamed and corroded like

10

the badlands east of Santa Fe" — or "he could see the sky, like a pale green sea rolling over the world."

One wonders at Savage's failure to obtain a permanent and enthusiastic audience since his demise. A number of reasons account for it. One is doubtless his sudden vanishing from the literary scene after his early death. Publishers are hesitant to promote deceased writers unless they've had a protracted and outstanding period of production, such as those of Zane Grey, Max Brand, Ernest Haycox, Luke Short. Savage's novelistic career spanned only ten years, from 1949's *TREASURE OF THE BRASADA* to 1959 when his agent suppressed his final novel and had Dudley Dean rewrite it (fortunately it was published in 1993 as Savage wrote it, titled *TABLE ROCK*).

I'd venture what I believe to be another major factor — perhaps a gift, but also a handicap in his time. Savage's characters are given to lots of introspective self-analysis, further complicated by their intricate relationships with others. This may be rather common in today's Western fiction, but in the

1950s it struck a sour chord with Western readers accustomed to far more simplistic and pruned-down treatments of protagonists. Novels like Walter Van Tilburg Clark's *THE OX-BOW INCIDENT* or MacKinlay Kantor's *WICKED WATER* were still "psychological" Westerns. They were alien to popular preferences. Savage's people were almost painfully Freudian (in 1862!?).

Les Savage, Jr., died in 1958 at the relatively youthful age of thirty-five — perhaps as much from the fiercely unslackening drive of his creative energies as from an official diagnosis of hereditary diabetes and elevated cholesterol. Yet in less than a decade he turned out twenty-four novels of the West, published under his own name and two pseudonyms (Logan Stewart and Larabie Sutter), including his memorable historicals of ambitious length, *SILVER STREET WOMAN* and *THE ROYAL CITY*. Before that, his output produced a fantastic number of short novels and short stories written for the pulp magazines of the 1940s, some of which have been collected in *SIX-GUN BRIDE OF THE TETON BUCH AND OTHER STORIES. FIRE DANCE*

AT SPIDER ROCK is a prime example of Savage's gifts displayed to their full advantage during his peak years.

Chapter One

There was no moon and Rim Fannin cursed thickly as he stumbled through the sooty blackness of the Tucson alley. Reaching its end, he could vaguely make out the ancient adobe wall surrounding the town. He paused, listening. From somewhere behind him a baby squalled and a woman scolded in Spanish. That was all.

Rim found a pebble on the ground and threw it against the mud wall. In a moment someone asked: "*¿Quien es?*"

"Rim Fannin."

There was a gap in the crumbling wall, a few feet to the right of the alley mouth. A figure materialized there, stepping through. In the black night, Rim had no more than a sense of a tall, narrow man, and of the immense straw sombrero he wore. The man stopped beside him, talking in Spanish: "You were not followed?"

Rim answered in Spanish. "I was careful, Archuleta."

"This is it then," Archuleta murmured. "I saw the wagons. Twenty of them I counted. Traveling by night toward Tubac. Always by night."

"White Mountain wagons?"

"I know not."

"What freight?"

"I know not. There were outriders, heavily armed. I tried to approach and they fired. They warned me away."

"That is all?"

"It is all I can tell you. The Portuguese said you would pay ten dollars for the information."

Rim fished in his pocket, pulled out silver. Archuleta took it, felt of it carefully, bit it, finally tucked it away. Without another word he turned and slipped back through the gap in the wall. Rim stood motionless for a time. The baby was wailing again. Rim thought there was no sound quite so miserable as that of a baby wailing in the night.

In strange counterpoint to that sound, as from a great distance he thought he caught soft tinkling, like the jangle of bracelets on a woman's wrist. He tried to identify it, but it stopped, and the baby stopped.

He started back through the alley,

stumbling once more in the litter of trash. At its far end a yellow river of light spilled from an open window. Rim could not avoid crossing it. Ducking low, he took it in two long strides. They brought him out into the street and he kept going down the block. At the corner he stopped with his back against the dank adobe wall of a house. From within came sleepy movements and a soft snoring. Then he heard the tinkling again.

A furtive motion touched that river of light through which Rim had passed. It resolved itself into a man. The barbaric jangle of bracelets accompanied his slightest movement, and silver glittered everywhere on his body as he stepped through the light. Then he was hidden by blackness, as Rim was hidden, and the sound stopped. Rim waited, holding his breath. After a long while, the tinkle began again, like the jingle of little bells, moving away from Rim, along the street.

When the sound died, Rim expelled his breath, grimacing. How the hell had he got into this? Life was hard enough without making yourself a hunted man.

He wheeled around the corner and

picked his way uncertainly up the Calle Real. It was more a filthy alley than a Royal Street, meandering its haphazard way through the wretched flat-roofed buildings of mud and thatch. For Tucson in this October of 1862 was a town of little more than a thousand souls, a lonely, white outpost surrounded by hundreds of square miles of hostile Indians. Most of the federal troops had been withdrawn for service in the war. Communication was completely cut off much of the time. Eastward the Apaches had stopped all Butterfield traffic and had laid waste to the stage stations; to the north the Navajos were raiding and plundering. Refugees entered Tucson daily with word of new massacres.

The fear could be felt in the Calle Real that night. Every man Rim saw went heavily armed and most of them moved in groups as if seeking the safety of numbers. In front of White Mountain Freight a line of parked Murphy wagons blocked the way, their mules fretting and snorting in creaking harnesses. Between a pair of wagons Rim saw the office door open and light silhouetted a woman's figure. That would be Sherry

17

Landor. A man rose up from the seat of a Murphy, light glittering on his rifle, and asked, "Who's there?"

"Rim Fannin."

The man bent to peer at Rim, satisfied himself, sank back into his seat. Rim ducked around the lead mules and walked toward Sherry. She'd heard him speak his name and had stopped with the door half closed behind her. There was something intensely Thoroughbred about Sherry Landor. Tall, slim, delicately boned of face and hand, with long blonde hair as silken and fine as sun mist. The ripeness of her lips and of her proud full bosom was a surprising contrast to her almost painful refinement, hinting at currents of womanliness and compassion hidden beneath the surface. And she was the only woman Rim knew who seemed comfortable in a hoop skirt.

" 'Evening, Sherry."

"Hardly a night to be wandering, Rim."

"A little drink here, a little drink there."

She did not answer, but in the compression of her full lips he saw her censure. It made him smile more broadly. The light revealed him now, six feet and 180 pounds of black Irish. Curly hair, so black it looked blue, black eyes, a clay-blue stain that would never leave the pale flesh of his long jaw no matter how often he shaved. On his broad shoulders was a shabby clawhammer coat and he wore his faded kerseymere trousers stuffed carelessly into jack boots with their tops folded down.

"Uncle Wylie's looking for you," she said. "He has a place on one of his wagons."

"I signed a pledge," he said ironically, "never to touch a dollar sullied by the blood of my comrades in the field."

She had eyes that could look ice blue or almost black, according to the light and her temper at the moment. They looked ice blue now. "You haven't given us much chance, have you?"

He said softly, "You didn't give us much chance."

Color stained her delicate cheekbones. She wore a wool spencer against the chill of the desert winds, and she pulled it more tightly about her body, as though withdrawing from him. "I'm through arguing with you," she said. "I, for one, don't see that Uncle Wylie did anything wrong. You would have seen that a year ago. You've changed so. You're so wild, so bitter."

And so confused, he thought. Suddenly he didn't want this between them any more. There had been a time when they had laughed together. He reached out and grasped her arms. The satiny warmth of her flesh stole through the spencer and seemed to burn his palms. She took a sharp breath. The blood was thick in his throat.

"Rim," she said.

For just a moment he saw perplexity in her eyes, and hope, a need of him as strong as his need of her. But when he tried to draw her to him, her face went taut and bleak, her whole body stiffened. This was the old rejection, the old propriety, holding him at arms' length, rising up at the slightest attempt at intimacy. It was worse than ever, with this new antagonism between them. The thickening of blood in his throat was desire no longer. It was anger, at Sherry, at the people and the country, at the culture that had made her this way. He let his hands slide off and stepped back. At the same moment the rear door of the office opened and Wylie

20

Landor entered from the freight yards, blinking in the lamplight.

"Sherry? That you?"

"Yes, Uncle Wylie." Her voice was stiff and tight. She moved away from Rim till she stood against the wall by the half-open door. There was a strained pallor to her face. "Rim's here."

Sherry's uncle came to the door, carrying a sheaf of papers in one slender hand. He was a tall, stooped man with snowy white hair, cropped short on his bony head. He wore a white shirt and a cheap suit, narrow-shouldered and ill-fitting, frayed at the cuffs, but always immaculate. He had flinty eyes, sunken cheeks that appeared tinged with gray. The precise grooves bracketing his thin, bloodless lips always seemed to convey a chronic disapproval of life. He looked at Sherry's face.

"It's after nine, Sherry."

"Yes, Uncle Wylie." She was looking at Rim. Her lips grew full and soft; a frown made its feathery tracing on her brow. Then she turned and walked away. Landor smiled mechanically at Rim.

"Come in. Give us a chance to talk, at least."

Rim hesitated. Then, with a long, angry stride, he went into the room. It was filled with the familiar litter and smells of a freighting office: harnesses and wheel bolts and packing cases heaped into a corner, the air pungent with the reek of wheel dope and sour leather. Landor nodded at one of the chairs and Rim sprawled into it, studying his muddy boots. Landor paced to the window, hands locked behind him, looking out at nothing. Rim glanced at the man's stiff neck, his high, narrow shoulders. Rim had always liked the old skinflint, Puritan and prude though he was. There was a heart behind that disapproving face, and Landor had been the best friend of Rim's father.

"I wish you'd try to see it clearer," Landor said.

"All I see is you've signed on with a snake," Rim said. "When the enemy occupies a town, a man don't stay in business unless he makes a deal."

Landor's hands knotted tighter. "There was no proof against Romaine. When the Confederates occupied Tucson, most of his rolling stock was out of town. I didn't see one pound of rebel freight move out of his yards."

"What about Dad? Who tipped the rebels off about Dad?"

Landor shook his head like a ringy old bull. "A hundred men in this town could have done that."

"But it was John Romaine who profited. He was just a shoestring freighter till they killed Dad. Now look."

Landor wheeled on him. "Rim, we've been over this a hundred times. I promised myself I wouldn't start it again. You've come back hurt and bitter and disillusioned. War will do that to a young man. It smashes a lot of ideals, changes his values, leaves him restless."

Rim rose, unable to sit still any longer. "It's more than that, Wylie. Something's going on. Something big and bad. And Romaine's in on it. Did you send an outfit south this week?"

The abrupt shift surprised Landor. "No."

"Twenty wagons, traveling at night, heading past Tubac?"

"Where did you get that?"

"Archuleta."

"That cutthroat!"

"He knows what's going on."

"And they'd hang him if he set foot in

23

town. How can you believe a man like that?"

"The same way you believe Romaine. He made a deal with the Confederates, and he's still up to something."

"Up to what?"

Rim lowered his head till his eyes were in shadow, gleaming like coals from a cave. "Don't you know?"

Landor went pale about the mouth. "I've taken all I'm going to. You've moped around town ever since you got back, bitter because you couldn't do anything about the war, carousing, raising hell, drinking. . . ."

"And you don't like a drunkard."

Landor's lips drew up like the mouth of a purse. It gave his face a severely Puritanical look. Somehow it symbolized for Rim the things that had shaped Sherry, made her the way she was.

"No," Landor said precisely, "I do not."

"Didn't you ever raise hell, Wylie?"

Landor's walk became mincing as he moved to the desk. "I called you in to give you another chance, Rim. A train is moving out for the Pima agency tomorrow. We need a driver."

"You're asking me to work for the man who killed my father, Wylie?"

Landor's lips grew thin and pale. He walked stiffly around the desk. The scarred swivel chair let out a protesting squawk as he sat down. He folded his pale clerk's hands decisively on the desk, staring at them.

"Very well, Rim. That's all."

Chapter Two

Rim walked to the end of the block and then stopped, easing his weight off his left leg. It was beginning to ache again, and his face turned gaunt with the bitterness that always came with the pain. He'd got the wound in August of last year, at the Second Bull Run, and they'd invalided him home after four months in the hospital. But the bitterness was more than the wound, more than that of a man uprooted and hurt and disillusioned by war. The real disillusionment had not come till his return home. Seeing a town run by a man like Romaine, who had played both ends against the middle, dealing with Unionist and Secessionist alike and growing fat off the profits. Seeing old friends accept such a rule without question, scrambling avidly for the leavings, simpering and servile as a bunch of court fools. Was that what a man fought for?

He started walking again, crossing the street, heading for the distant lights of the Domingo Saloon. Halfway down the block, in the darkness of an overhang, he stopped again. The Murphy wagons had begun to move from in front of the White Mountain Freight office. They passed him out in the night, with the husky voices of the drivers, the creak of great wheels, the tinkle of bit chains. Or was it bit chains? He strained to make out the shapes of the wagons, but they remained a mere smoky stirring in the moonless night, an unseen rumbling of immense freighters that made the earth tremble beneath his feet.

Cautiously he started walking again. He sensed the mouth of an alley just ahead. And he heard that tinkling again.

This time he swung till his back was against the blank front of the building. He put his hand on the butt of the Navy .36 holstered on his hip. He had been expecting this for weeks now, from Romaine, and he thought it was about time.

He heard the barbaric jangling again, closer, on his right. It turned his head that way. From the mouth of the alley at his left there was a sudden rush of boots. He turned back and pulled his gun and waited till he saw the figure, bursting from the alley and wheeling toward him. Then, deliberately, viciously, face high, he whipped the gun at the man.

He felt its barrel bite into the solidity of flesh and bone. The man screamed in pain and came helplessly against Rim with all his weight. Rim gagged on the musty smell of wool and sweat and whiskey. He tried to shove the man's slack, sodden body off, but he was too late. The second one was on Rim from the other side.

He sensed the blow coming and automatically threw up his left arm. The blow crushed his forearm against his face and flung him staggering into the alley. He tripped and fell and tried to roll away, still gripping his gun. The movement of a man filled the alley mouth and he took a snap shot at him. But he must have missed, for the man reached him before he could rise.

A boot cracked into his ribs and he shouted with pain. His gun was kicked from his hand and then another kick struck him in the head. The world exploded and he flopped over like an animal in panic, trying to get away.

He heard the stamp of boots follow him and lashed out with his feet. He felt a leg and scissored his ankles, tripping the man. But the one he had pistol-whipped must have recovered, for Rim again heard the sound of stumbling boots on the baked earth, and again his body rocked to a kick. They were both on him then, kicking, slugging, stamping. Pain filled his mind like clotted wool and his muscles would not respond to his will.

Then, from a mile above him, he heard a cracking gunshot and a wild shout. There was a second sharp detonation. The kicks stopped; the earth of the alley trembled to running boots, the gasp of driven breathing. After that a voice floated in to Rim from halfway round the world.

"Whyn't you stick around, you damn va'mints? I'll give you the mos' eleegant hidin' you evah had."

Rim rolled over, groaning softly. Vision returned in speckled flashes. He could hear the receding drum of running boots and he sat up against the wall, hugging his ribs, and tried to see. He had an unreal glimpse of a figure passing through the backwash of light in front of the Domingo. All he could see were flailing boots and the broad back of a calico vest. Then he became aware of the man standing beside him. In one hand he held a coiled bull whip. Rim realized that it hadn't been gunshots he had heard — it had been the crack of twenty-four feet of cured leather, tipped with a popper made from the belt buckle of a Union cavalry officer. The man spoke again, in a voice as Southern as hominy grits and Kentucky redtop.

"Lonesome, fetch that bull's-eye over heah and let's see if they left anythin' alive."

A man tramped from a halted Murphy wagon, a bull's-eye lantern swinging in one hand. Its light crept up the figure standing over Rim, revealing a tall, lanky youth with corn-yellow hair and a sharp-featured, hungry-looking face. He had only one arm, and the empty sleeve of his gray tunic was folded up and pinned to his shoulder. When he saw Rim he swore.

"Damn it, I thought it was some thievin' Injun tryin' to hamstring one of our skinners again. I'd o' known it was a damnyankee, I'd o' let 'em have your hide, and welcome to it."

Rim shook his head, trying to clear the wool out. It sent a stab of pain against his eyes. He squinted them shut. "What's a Johnny Reb like you doing out here?"

"Occupyin' the town for Sherod Hunter till he comes back," the man said.

The man with the lantern stopped before them. Rim saw that it was Lonesome, a bullwhacker who had driven for his father before the war. Lonesome was a stooped, snaggle-toothed man in his middle fifties with a face seamed and corroded like the badlands east of Santa Fe. He wiped a hand absently across pale blue eyes, habitually watering from a lifetime in the biting winds of the desert. Then he indicated the one-armed man.

"This is Steve Swan, Rim. He was with Sherod Hunter when the rebels took the town. Lost his arm when Barret hit Hunter in Picacho Pass. Been paroled to us for a driver."

Rim got to his feet, grimacing at the dull spasm of pain it caused him. "Burnside will probably court-martial

31

me," he told Swan, "but I thank you anyway."

Swan grinned. "If you won't tell Gen'ral Lee, I'll accept. What'd they have ag'in you anyway, Yank?"

Rim looked down the street, remembering the calico vest. "Calico Mills still work for Romaine?" he asked Lonesome.

The old man nodded. "He's outrider f'r this very train."

Rim turned to him. "Did you know Landor asked me to sign on?"

"Sure," Lonesome said. "We all did. Romaine's having a bad time gettin' a driver f'r this Pima run."

A malicious grin curled at Rim's mouth. "Lonesome, there's only one thing that would make me take the job."

"What?"

"If I thought Romaine was trying to keep me from it."

The White Mountain Freight yards were behind the line of buildings on the Calle Real, really no more than a hard-packed flat ringed with ocotillo corrals for the stock and lines of parked Murphys. Most of the Pima train had been wheeled into the yards by the time Rim got there, riding Lonesome's wagon. The place was a madhouse of braying, kicking mules and cursing skinners and laboring swampers. As soon as Lonesome pulled to a halt, two Papago swampers had the tail gate down and were heaving sacks of flour into the musty bed.

Rim climbed stiffly from the high seat, favoring his wounded leg, and trailed Lonesome through the maze of teams and freighters and men to the wagon boss' rig. Here, in the ruddy light of a lantern, stood the owner of White Mountain, John Romaine, talking with one of his skinners.

A big man, Romaine was, bluff and hearty and well met, a follower of politics, a quoter of the latest foul joke, a back-slapper in the barbershop and a center of interest in the saloon, a wearer of fine broadcloth and a drinker of fine whiskey. He had tawny hair and a broad, good-natured face and twinkling blue eyes. Everything about him seemed blunt and foursquare and forthright. It took a long acquaintance before a man started to look for the crevices of guile at the tips of his eyes, the spurious geniality in his expansive good humor. He saw Rim's torn coat, the blood and grime caked on his face, and frowned concernedly.

"Looks like somebody fed you a dose of tanglefoot again, son," he said.

Rim resented that "son". He was only three years younger than Romaine. "Landor told me you needed another driver," he said.

Romaine chuckled. "You?"

"Why not?"

"That leg."

"I can whip just as good from a seat."

Romaine's blunt-fingered hands were always moving, fingering his handsome gold watch chain, stroking the lapel of his tailored clawhammer, touching his silken burnsides. He made Rim think of a man who wanted to pick up everything in the room and put it in his pocket.

"You're a little late, anyway, son," Romaine said, still grinning. "We've got our driver."

Another man came around the stern of the wagon in time to hear him. "What the hell you talkin' about, Romaine?" he said. "I scoured the bottom of the barrel. There ain't another driver in a thousand miles."

Rim turned to see Yaki Peters, Romaine's wagon boss. He had recently gained fame by hauling a load through the sheer suicide of Apache Pass when no other skinner would attempt it. He was a massive, rawboned giant in linsey-woolsey jeans held up by a pair of snakeskin galluses. Long red underwear sufficed for his shirt, stained by sweat and liquor and wheel dope. There was something equine to the heavy bones of his face. Blue-veined lids drooped deeply over his hazel eyes, giving them a hooded look.

It seemed an effort for Romaine to keep his humor. "We don't need that extra wagon," he said.

Yaki stopped before them. He carried his thirty-foot mule whip coiled about his neck, the handle hanging down one side, the popper on the other. He grasped these two tails as a man would grasp the lapels of his coat. A livid scar ran from the square joint of his right thumb to the outside of the hand, severing the sinews of index and middle fingers so that they stood out stiff and helpless from the others. He met Rim's eyes for a moment, a sullen light kindling in his hazel eyes.

Then he looked at Romaine.

"You better not short them Pimas this time," he said. "You'll have an uprising on your hands."

Romaine frowned. Finally he shook his head. "No," he said, "I don't think we need him."

"I think we do," Yaki said. Romaine looked sharply at him. Something seemed to pass between the two men. Yaki spoke softly. "I say we sign him on."

A dull flush ran into Romaine's face. Then he made an impatient gesture with one hand. "It's your string. Do what you like. I have an appointment."

He glanced at Rim, then wheeled and moved away. Men gathered to him as he walked and he clapped one on the back and his genial laugh boomed up over the other sounds.

"A strange power you have over Romaine," Rim said. "I never saw him back down before."

Yaki grinned balefully at Rim. Then he nodded across the yard. "You'll take Number Ten, right behind Lonesome. You know how I drive. Toe the mark or git the sack. We're moving out at dawn."

Rim nodded and went toward the

wagon. Dodging a six-hitch team that was being backed into its traces, he glanced ruefully at his torn and dirty clawhammer. He would need more serviceable clothes than that; there were rawhide britches and a mackinaw at home. He found Number Ten at the edge of the yards, the only rig that wasn't being loaded. He was looking around for swampers when the woman passed through the light of the lantern hanging on the stern of Lonesome's wagon. Rim saw that it was Corsica Bartlett, half-breed daughter of a Navajo squaw and a white whiskey drummer. Morally she had inherited all that was bad in both parents; physically she had inherited all that was good. Her hair was jet black and so sleek it looked wet. Her face was a piquant oval of exotic beauty, with big black eyes that danced with devilment. Her body held all the lush excitement of some desert flower, blooming with a brief and savage beauty that was des- tined to die too soon. She wore the blue velvet tunic of the Navajo woman, dar- ingly unbuttoned below her throat. The voluminous, flowered skirt would have hidden another woman from the waist down, but every movement she made seemed calculated to draw it tight against the opulent swell of hip, the outer curve of thigh. She stopped before him, smelling faintly of sage and some wild perfume. A fey smile touched her coral-red lips. Then it faded and something brooding sought the hollows of her cheeks.

"I hear Landor ask you to drive," she said.

"Not many men have such a delicious good-bye," he said.

She moved closer. Her cannel-coal earrings glittered like jet in the back-wash of the lantern. The voluptuous curves of her body were inches from him and the passionate promise of her crept against him like musk, stirring his blood. He looked down at the pale oval of her face, filled with the bitter-sweet knowledge that this had become his world now. The harlots and the drunks and the saloons. Once he had known another world, where a woman didn't show her body so blatantly, where a man had no cause to drink himself into a stupor night after night, where friends were honored and re-spected in town. But he had come back to find all that changed. Respectability had changed places with shame. The goodness of a woman was no longer his; the decency of friends was veiled behind hypocrisy. The harlots and the drunks and the lost ones were the only honest people left because they admitted what they were and sought no profit from the blood of their brothers. It was a crazy irony, and he suddenly wanted to laugh. She saw the corners of his eyes crinkle and anger flushed her face.

"You laugh at me?"

He caught her arms. "No, Corsica. I cry for you. I cry for all the poor fools who ever believed in anything or thought an ideal was worth dying for."

"You always talk crazy, Reem. I no come here to hear that."

"You came to tell me good-bye. A kiss, a tear, a fond farewell."

"Don't go."

"What?"

"Don't go," she repeated. She brought all the silken softness of her body against him, twining her arms about his neck. It was a long kiss, savage-sweet. It was the kind of thing that could drive a man crazy. "Come home with me," she murmured. "Don't go."

Her lips slid up his cheek to his ear and back to his cheek again. He was holding her so tightly he knew it hurt and yet she made no sound of pain. Finally he knew he would go with her if they didn't quit and he pulled himself away, laughing shakily.

"A few days," he said. "I'll be back in a few days."

"Now." Something intense had entered her voice. She sought to pull herself against him once more. "Come with me now. Don't go."

The strange feverishness of her tone made him hold her away, looking into her eyes. "Corsica, what's the matter?"

"I don't want you to go."

"Don't tell me you'll miss me that bad." Their relationship had always been casual and gay and tacitly under-stood before.

"I will," she said.

"No," he said. "This is something new and you know it. You've got a reason. Do you know something?"

He tried to look in her eyes but she forced her body against him again, face against his chest, voice half muffled by his coat. "Reem, please don't go. I just want you to stay here."

40

"Do you know something? Is it about Romaine?"

"Reem, please, please!"

"Is this train running into trouble? Corsica, you've got to tell me."

She started to answer. But something beyond him caught her attention. A look of fear touched her face and, with a muffled sound, she pulled away and ran back through the wagons. Rim started to follow, then checked himself, wheeling to see what she had been looking at.

There was a man standing between two Murphys, fifty feet away. In the darkness he was unrecognizable, like a malignant shadow hovering there. He watched Rim for a moment longer, then turned and walked into the maze of animals. Just before he disappeared, he passed through a cone of light cast by a lantern, and Rim saw who it was.

Yaki Peters.

Chapter Three

They lined out at dawn, taking the Calle Real through the huddle of gray and ghostly buildings to where the ancient wall — built in Spanish colonial times as protection against the Indians — surrounded the town. Outside the wall the street became a wagon road, leading northward along the sluggish Santa Cruz River to the Pima villages. The pungent reek of greasewood after a recent rain was everywhere and, as soon as the sun flushed the sky, they could see the land stretching out before them, frighteningly vast, incredibly empty. The sun was pale and the chill ate into a man's bones.

Rim sat high on the wagon box, huddled into his father's mackinaw. Beside him was his swamper, Jonathan Street, a towhead from New England. He was a slow-witted, garrulous youth who talked endlessly of nothing and Rim hardly heard half of what he said. The groan of harness and the miserable shriek of iron-tired wheels and the husky cursing of the skinners seemed to be the only real sounds in the world. A pall of dust sifted up from the turning wheels, hanging over the train so thickly that Rim could hardly see Lonesome's wagon ahead of them.

At the noon halt there was little time for talk. While the cook was readying the grub, the drivers were greasing their wheels. It was back-breaking labor, jacking up the immense freighters, pulling the linchpins, removing the wheels. But they had to be checked at every stop or a hot box would develop from the fine sand that was lifted and deposited on the axle at every turn of the wheel. After that the teams were watered, and then they had fifteen minutes for fried bacon, half-cooked beans, and charred sourdough. Rim had just enough time to scour his tin cup and plate with sand and ashes when the time-honored order came ringing down the line: *"Stri-i-ing out!"*

The dust again, the rattle and clash of stay chains, four thousand pounds of freight shifting and groaning in the great oak beds. Already Rim's body ached with the hammering it had taken on the high seat. This first day, before things were shaken down, a man always wondered why he stuck with it. Yet there was a pull to the trail he couldn't ignore, once he'd had a taste of it. Rim's father, in the latter days before his death, had made enough to retire if he'd wanted to. Yet he couldn't quit, and was out bossing his trains half the time himself.

In the late afternoon the wind began blowing and the dust swept against them in choking clouds. Rim dropped off the wagon on the lee side of the team, where he had some protection. He saw Lonesome trudging by his wagon ahead, and joined him. The old man wiped dust from the furrows of his grizzled face, giving Rim a sour look.

"I s'pose you still think I'm sellin' out."

"You know how I feel about Romaine."

Lonesome dabbed at watering eyes. "A man gits old, Rim. He only knows how to do one thing. He's gotta eat. What's he do, with only one freighter in town?"

"He could go to another town," Rim said. "I thought I knew what I was fighting for when I went away, Lonesome. Now, I don't know anything.

You let a man like this go on, day after day, not touching him, not trying to stop him. . . ."

"Stop him from what?"

"Everything. What about the Pima beef?"

"Archuleta rustled it."

"Archuleta doesn't operate that far north. Romaine got his government money, didn't he? It's a typical operation. Ten bucks he turned around and sold that beef to the Salt River mines. So Romaine makes his double profit and the Pimas get sick of being cheated and used and they rise up like the Navajos, and a company of soldiers goes out to stop 'em and half the soldiers get killed so Romaine can go on getting bigger watches and fancier buggies."

Rim stopped, angered at his own bitterness. It seemed useless to be bitter again. Maybe getting drunk was better, after all.

Lonesome shook his head. "You ain't got no proof, son. I think it all goes back to your dad. You blame Romaine for that and it taints everything else you see."

Rim did not answer. Lonesome rubbed a fist at his watering eyes and tramped back up to his creaking wagon, climbing aboard. They were passing a broad loop in the Santa Cruz now. Indian Swing, they called it. Rim stopped a moment, looking out at the low bottomlands encroaching on the tobacco-brown river. This was where his father had been found. This was where Sean Fannin had been found, in February of 1862, with his shirt torn from his back and his dead body lacerated and scarred as though from Indian torture.

Rim had been fighting in the East at the time, but Wylie Landor had written him the terrible news. The beginning of it, actually, had been in March of 1861. A huge shipment of Harper's Ferry rifles and ammuni-tion had arrived at Fort Buchanan, just south of Tucson, to replace the obsolete arms of all the troops in the territory. Before the guns could be distributed, Fort Sumter fell, and the war had begun.

All federal troops were ordered to evacuate the territory for service in the East. Sean Fannin, the biggest shipper in the area, was given the contract of hauling the Harper's Ferries. The guns were a prize coveted by the Confederates, however, who were moving up the Rio Grande in a large force. With his troops scattered and not ready for battle, the Union commander did not want to risk the guns; he ordered Fannin to make a run for it to Fort Yuma, where the California Column was forming.

On February 27, 1862, Sean Fannin left Tucson with thirty wagons. But Captain Sherod Hunter and his Texas cavalry were already moving on Tucson. Somehow Hunter found out the route Fannin was taking and caught him at Indian Swing. Rim's father put up a fight. There was evidence that he had tried to burn his wagons. And he had died for it.

Looking out at the river, Rim was remembering the tall, black-haired, laughing god of a man that he had worshipped. Would Sean Fannin think his son a fool now? Was Lonesome right? Was all this hatred of Romaine founded upon the sands of hearsay and false bitterness? Rim shook his head helplessly. Someone had killed his father. Someone other than Sherod Hunter or his men.

A shout from Rim's swamper jerked

him out of his reverie. He saw that the wagon had passed him and was a hundred yards ahead. Street was hauling on the jerk line and snapping his whip awkwardly at the mules.

"Git up here, Rim. They're headin' inter that bog. I can't turn 'em."

Running forward to the wagon, Rim saw that the rain had turned a dip in the road into a muddy bog. The other wagons had veered around it; he could still see their wheel tracks circling the mud and crossing the high, hard ground west of the bog. But Street, probably asleep on the seat, had let their team walk right into it, plodding up to their knees. Rim knew a raw anger at the youth. Then he cursed himself for it, because he was as much to blame as the swamper.

The mud was chuckling and popping triumphantly about the wheels of the wagon. Rim ran for its head, wincing every time he put his weight on his bad leg. He grabbed wildly for the jerk line, giving a violent tug.

"Gee, Patches, gee, Indian. Gee, you jug-headed canaries!"

The nigh leader wheeled right so hard he almost upset his mate. One by one

48

the spans floundered from the deeper mud onto firm ground at one side, until it came to the swingers, just ahead of the tongue. Rim loosed his whip, cracking it above the near swinger's rump. The hairy black mule stumbled over its taut pull chain in an effort to swing the tongue right. The whole front of the wagon jerked as the animal hit its collar. The wheelers squealed and the hardwood tree groaned and gave, turning slightly in the bog.

"Gee, you bag of bones! Point that tree, swing 'er 'round, gee-up, gee-up!"

The pointers were grunting and squealing against their collars in the battle to turn the tongue farther right, but it would not budge. With Rim's attention on the hind spans, the leaders had got too far out to the right, and their lusty pulling threw one of the pointers off balance, spilling him into the mud.

"Haw! Haw!" bawled Rim. But he was so excited now that his pull on the line was neither long nor steady. The leaders mistook it for the double jerk of an off turn, driving farther toward the right in their collars. This pulled the other pointer off balance. He went down, kicking and braying, fouling the jerk line up so that Rim lost all control over the leaders. Still turning right, they began jackknifing back on the hind spans. In excited frenzy, the downed pointers kicked and bit, and the reaction spread clear down the line. Lonesome had halted his wagon up ahead now and was running back to help.

"Get those pointers on their feet, Rim. I'll try to shove these leaders back into line," he called.

Rim was down in the mud now. He danced around outside the kicking hoofs of the off-swinger till he could duck in and grab its bit, yanking the biting head around and pulling up on it. A glancing kick sent him spinning before he could force the animal up. He pulled himself out of the mud, wiping it off his face, circling back in to grab the bit again. Another hoof lashed out, and he reeled back. The air was filled with a bedlam of screaming, hee-hawing mules. In a fit of anger, he shook his whip out again. He had played around long enough. Instead of cracking the popper above their heads, he laid it right into the wheeler. The off-animal leaped forward under the lash, trampling the swinger's flailing hind legs.

"Don't burn them like that," called Lonesome. "You'll whip them right out of the harness, boy. Don't lose your head."

Rim could hardly hear him. The off-swinger, fighting to get from beneath the wheeler's forehoofs, scrambled erect into the next mule's hind hoofs. That animal began braying and kicking, knocking the wheeler back. Rim turned the whip on him, trying to keep him off while the wheeler got up. All the spans were in a veritable orgy of braying and squealing and kicking and biting. Rim flayed them with indiscriminate wrath, shouting frenziedly.

"You damn, stubborn, sop-and-taters fools, pull straight at least! Can't you see what you're doing? I'll take the hide off your rumps and stuff it down your throats till you choke, you goddam sonofa. . . ."

The whip was no longer in his hand. Before he realized why, some unseen force clutched his shoulder. He shouted with the pain of it. He was spun around, fighting to pivot rather than fall. Then he was thrown back so hard he could no longer keep his balance and went

51

stumbling and falling to his hands and knees in the black mud.

Yaki Peters stood six feet away, holding in one hand the whip he had taken from Rim, regarding him with those heavy-lidded, somnolent eyes. Rim's face twisted and he made a strangled, inarticulate sound down in his throat, lunging to rise.

"Boy!" It was Lonesome's voice, and Lonesome's hand on his shoulder, the pressure momentarily forcing him down. "You don't want to do that now. He'll hide you with that whip if you do. He'll kill you. . . ."

"I'm glad you decided to stay down there a spell," said Yaki. "I think you got a few things to learn about mules. They're ladies and gentlemen, just like anybody else. Especially fine, blue-blooded Missouri mules like these." He rolled a juicy gob around in his mouth and spat with great emphasis. "I think you got something to learn about this whip, too. It ain't there to burn them up every time they gee instead of haw. It's your badge of authority, like a peace officer. All you got to do is show it to them once in a while to prove your right to give them orders."

He dropped Rim's whip and turned to the team. He reached up to grab his own blacksnake in that habitual way, like a man hanging on to the lapels of his coat, one hand on either end of the thirty foot whip slung around his neck and trailing on the ground.

"Gentlemen," he said, without raising his voice much. The excited team went on braying and kicking, ears laid back, teeth bared, the whole line heavy, swaying, jerking. Yaki grabbed the stock of the whip in his right hand. Holding it, with those two helpless fingers thrust out, he raised it above his head where every mule in the line could see it. Then, with his left hand, he reached up and wrapped those two stiff fingers around the whipstock so they gripped the handle along with the three good ones.

"That's it," whispered Lonesome, in an awed voice.

Still trembling with the effort to control his rage, Rim did not realize what had happened for a moment. Then it reached him. The noise had stopped. Everything had stopped. Rim could not believe it. The off-swinger, still down, lay on his side in a ludicrous posture, one leg still in mid-air, the whites of his eyes gleaming in solemn, comical attention as he stared at Peters.

"They've worked with Yaki before, I guess," cackled Lonesome.

"Now ain't you ashamed of yourselves, making me show my authority that-away," said Yaki. The wheelers actually hung their heads. A recalcitrant leader, in a last gesture of defiance, jumped across a tug chain to bite at his companion. "Young man!" snapped Yaki, turning to point the whipstock at him. The mule leaped back over the chain with great alacrity and stood there trying to look nonchalant. Yaki walked down to him and began untangling the jerkline. "You know better'n that, Senator Patches. A man in your position can't afford to act like a yearlin' coon any longer. Naow, as I see it, there ain't no call to rip your jeans over a job like this. Look at that dry ground to the right. You could walk across it dainty as a daisy, couldn't you? Well, this yere mud ain't no more than dry ground got a little wet."

He gave the animal an affectionate pat on the rump. The dun mule, blotched with black patches, had been standing with his head turned away from Yaki

54

but, as the man moved down to the next span, one white eye rolled around, following his figure in equine propitiation.

"Mule talk," Lonesome cackled under his breath. "What'd I tell you, boy, reg'lar old hardshell Baptist mule talk. If his ma was a hinny, his pa was a preacher, I swear. Listen now. He's going into the shortrows. You won't even be able to understand him in a minute. But those mules will. And they'll pull this outfit to the moon if he asks 'em."

Rim had almost forgotten his rage in the fascination of watching this. It was unbelievable. It was a parody on mule-skinning. It was a travesty.

"Don't be crazy," he muttered to Lonesome. "No man could get that outfit to dry ground now. It's up to the hubs in that bog. Not with a hundred mules."

"Hit's like the ole houn' dog when he's chasin' ole Zip coon an' ole Zip runs into a b'ar's cave," went on Yaki, walking down the spans of mules and freeing the jerkline at each one. His voice, however, was losing the soft, paternal drawl as he drew nearer the wagon. It had begun to rise, taking on the character of an exhortion, vehemence adding a forceful exhalation to the end of every

55

few words. "Ole Dan Tucker comes up to 'at b'ar's cave and he thinks hit's a b'ar in thar, hah! His tail sticks up straight as the ramrod on a Jake Hawkins and his ears p'in' right back to his tail, an' he won't move a mite, hah!"

As he reached the swing mule, his tone dropped momentarily to a husky confidence. "Now, Jonah, I think you been lying there in the mud long enough. How about getting up and helping ole Dan tree that coon. Here's a hand."

He slipped a scarred, bony hand beneath the mule's knee and helped him up with as much solicitude as a grandson righting an older relative. Then he moved on to the wheelers, his voice rising once more.

"Yessir. Ole Dan won't tree that coon, scairt to death hit's a b'ar, hah! Cain't move, hah! Cain't bark, hah! Thar's the Piker, hah, thar's old b'ar, hah! Naow ole Dan, you tell him, ole Dan, you know puttin' a snake in the barrel will sweeten the cider, that hain't no b'ar in thar, hit's only ole Zip coon, hah!"

His reversion to the dialect of original environments seemed to grow in ratio to the expanding volume of his voice, until he was shouting a hoarse, frenzied, barely coherent stream of colloquialism at the painfully attentive animals.

"But thar he stan's, Pig in the Parlor, laigs stiff as a fence rider. Ole Dan Tucker, late fer his supper, blister mah tongue if hit ain't, hah, an' he won't go past hit no matter what you do. So sweeten the cider, boot his tail, hah, git in thar, Dan, hit ain't nothin' but old Zip coon. And what does he do? He give a howl, bro-o-ah! An' in he goes, hah. An' that's the way this yere job looks to me. Mud's only wet dirt, hah. Ain't no b'ar in thar, only a coon. You can git past hit. I don't want to sweeten your cider, hah, but I will if I have to, hah. I got my badge right here on my arm and you seed it, so now I'm going to give you the bit-hah, and when I do, I want you to give a good strong pull, hah."

He had reached the brake, to which the jerkline was attached. The mules had stopped the nervous twitching of their tails. Their long ears were pointed straight up. Every animal in the line seemed to tense itself as if sensing the peak of his exhortation. Having heard his soft sibilant voice, Rim would never have believed him capable of even the hoarse volume his shouts had already attained, but that paled before the sudden roar emanating from him now.

"Bra-a-h, now, let's giddup, hah, bra-a-h, let's gee-ah. Gee-ah!"

It rolled out over the animals' heads in a command that deafened Rim, crackling with the raucous edge of a mule's bray, yet infinitely louder than any mule, filled with an ear-splitting clap of thunder, and having the same effect.

Harness broke into a creaking, popping protest, tug-chains rattled, then clinked into drawn-taut silence as all sixteen animals surged into their collars as one, grunting and straining in a concert of effort.

"Gee there, Patches, bra-a-ah!" He reared at them like some equine god. *"Giddap there, Methuselah, jump that tree, put the snake in the cider and keep it sweet, hah!"* Each mule was reacting as if he had stripped the hide from its rump with that unused whip. *"That's hit, Jonah, hit your hames, hah!"*

"He'll never do it," muttered Rim. "That outfit's stuck till the road's dry and then some."

Grunting, squealing, straining, the mules heaved against their collars in prodigious effort, Yaki's incantation driving them on like fiends in a jack-ass hell. But finally their concert began to crumble in the face of their utter failure to budge the Murphy and its trailer. The off-leader was first to break. Hoofs ploughing up the mud, he finally slipped and fell against his mate. The near animal jumped over its tug chain in an effort to maintain its balance.

"Patches!" It was as if the beast had bounced over the chain in reaction to Yaki's bellow. "You ain't forcing me to use my authority, are you?" The wagon boss raised that whipstock, reaching up as if to curl his two outthrust fingers in around it again. Eyes rolled white in jackass heads and sixteen desperate mules threw themselves in a wild, new effort at their ungiving collars, humping, straining, groaning with Missouri agony. Then Rim heard the first dog pop. *"That's hit,"* screamed Yaki, *"bra-a-h, gee-up, gee-up, gee-up!"*

For a moment the gargantuan yell drowned the popping wagon dogs. Then the small chortle of mud began, as the massive wheels moved. Hounds shrieked with the first tentative lash of the tongue toward the right. Then the wheels were rolling, dripping chocolate mud off three-inch iron tires into their own ruts. Yaki's bellowing became more frenetic as the Murphy lurched forward until, at last, nothing but a stream of incoherent gibberish, connected by great panting hah's was leaving his frothing lips.

"Gee-hah there, Patches, hah, bro-o-o-hah! Keep your chur, ah! Jump those tugs, Methuselah! Dan Tucker git no supper. Lookyear you one-gallus idjit, git that trailer, hah, before she dumps the whole outfit, hah."

Rim did not realize the last had been bellowed at him and Lonesome, till Lonesome ran by where he was still crouched, answering Yaki. "She'll go completely over if I unhitch her."

"I don't care, hah. I'll never get this Murphy moving again if I stop it for that trailer, hah! Knock that coupling out, hah, hit that collar, Patches, hit that collar, hah!"

Rim saw what they were yelling about now. As soon as the mules had turned the wagon to the right, it canted up on that side, climbing out of the bog onto higher, dry ground. That load must have shifted in the trailer, for it was tilting dangerously to the near side, tongue groaning on its coupling. Lonesome slopped into the mud, tearing the big axe from its place on the side of the wagon box and beating at the coupling bolt.

Then he jumped back, dropping the axe. The trailer's off-wheels pulled free of the mud with a great sucking sound and the vehicle capsized. Yaki was in a veritable paroxysm now, exhorting the mules into a final effort.

"Boo-o-ohah, hyah, come to the infair, gee-hah! Jonah, jump 'at tree, whetabanteronthatcradle, hah, gimme-oldtimereligion, hah! Jumpatstumb, watchertug, hyah! Tucker, hah! Don't quit now, hah! Hog up, hog up, corn bread and no butter, git thar, hah, you hain't no giglet at a rockin', hah! Jump 'at coon, hah, make handspike daylight, git hit, hah, keep yer chur, keep yer chur, hah! Chur, hah! Gidday, hah, gee-up, hah! Brayah! Hyyah! Broo-o-o-hah!"

Lonesome and Rim stood knee deep in mud watching the immense Murphy wagon lurch onto dry ground, halting there as Yaki stopped his team with a last explosive *who, hah!* Lonesome stared fixedly at the great, gaunt, awkward, red-shirted wagon boss standing on high ground with his long arms fallen limply to his sides, his whole body drooping in the abject let-down of a spent revivalist after his last hallelujah.

"Boy," Lonesome told Rim in hushed tones, "you have just seen a piece of mule-skinning."

Chapter Four

It seemed a long time before Yaki Peters lifted his rawboned shoulders, turned, and came back to Rim. He moved in a loose-jointed, slide-footed shuffle. He stopped in front of Rim, rubbing a sweaty palm against his red undershirt, blackened by the filth and spilled liquor and daubs of wheel dope he'd wiped off his hands.

"You'll lose a day's wages for that," he said. His voice sounded hoarse, spent. "Next time it happens, I'll hitch your wagon behind mine and you'll walk back to Tucson alone."

Rim felt a flush of anger and shame rise into his face. But he did not answer. There was nothing to say. He had committed one of the unpardonable sins of skinning. The other drivers had gathered around in a loose circle, watching silently. He wanted to crawl in a hole somewhere.

"Git that trailer righted now," Yaki said. "I'll give you an hour."

He wheeled and shambled back toward the head of the train. Little knots of muscle bulging along his jaw, Rim waded down into the mud. Lonesome joined him. They had to unload the trailer to right it.

"I'm glad you held your tongue," Lonesome said, heaving out a sack of flour. "Yaki is one man it don't pay to buck. See them two stiff fingers? He got the tendons cut by a skinner's whip in Missouri. Yaki whipped that skinner's face off." They carried a pair of sacks to high ground and dumped them. Lonesome wiped his sweating face. "And that puckered scar on his left palm? Some Mex in Austin pinned Yaki's hand to the wall with a knife. Yaki's whipstock is wrapped with strips o' that Mex's hide. I seen it happen. Yaki did the whole thing with that knife pinning his hand there against the wall. The Mex couldn't no more get away from Yaki's whip than a fly can get off flypaper."

They waded back to the trailer. "You're blowing," Rim said.

"That ain't no windy," Lonesome said. "God's truth. Yaki'll use that whip on a man quicker'n he'll do it on his mules. Only one way to get him. You gotta have a whip and you got to wait till Yaki tries for your head. Then you duck under his lash and wind your own snake around his legs. When he's down, you got him. I seen Whack Ellis try, but he wasn't fast enough. Yaki spilled him and broke his back when he was down."

"Whack Ellis didn't have no right to call himself a mule-skinner," said a drawling voice behind them. "He couldn't drive a sick mouse across a Davy Crockett log."

They turned to see Steve Swan standing in the mud.

"Where'd you know Whack?" Lonesome asked.

"Him and me hided many a mule together," the rebel said. "You want a hand?"

Rim tried not to look at the empty sleeve. "You'll lose your stripes," he said.

"They'll promote me," Swan said, "f'r showin' a damnyankee up by doin' twice as much with one wing as he can with two."

He was grinning when he said it. Rim couldn't help grinning back. He climbed into the wagon and pulled another sack down. "Take this one, then."

As he swung it towards Swan's shoulder, a corner caught on the tail gate. It unbalanced the sack and he had to let it go to keep its weight from pulling him over. The sack hit on the end of the bed and split open, spilling its contents out in a tawny stream. They all stood goggle-eyed, watching it dribble into the mud. It was sand. Rim hunkered down, running his fingers through it. He didn't find a bit of flour.

He looked up at Lonesome, at Swan. Then, without a word, he rose, took out his clasp knife, and slit another sack. More sand dribbled out. He climbed down into the mud and walked up to his Murphy, where Yaki had left it on high ground. He climbed into the seat and slit a sack on top of the load. Sand leaked into his palm. Lonesome and Swan had followed. He showed it to them. He looked at Lonesome.

"We'd better tell Yaki," Swan said. He went away toward the head of the train. Rim looked again at Lonesome, then dumped the sand from his hand.

"That's the man you're working for," he said.

Lonesome bridled. "How can you be so sure it's Romaine? This could go right back to the mill."

Rim saw Yaki coming back with Swan. The rest of the men had built a fire and were gathered around it, boiling a pot of coffee. They were not aware of what was going on. Yaki stopped by Rim's wagon, looking up at him. Rim reached in for another handful of sand, showed it to him. The wagon boss scowled, tugging at the whip coiled around his neck.

"This is a helluva thing," he said. "Let's not spread it to the others till we find out what it's all about. I'll ride back and tell Romaine."

"The Army ought to know about it," Rim said.

"Romaine'll probably take it up with them," Yaki said.

He started to go on but a shout from the head of the train checked him. Rim saw that most of the men about the campfire were on their feet. A rider was visible at a distance, approaching the train. He came in through the pear flats, his spavined roan veering and stumbling. He was a bearded, red-shirted man, bent forward over his saddle horn. Rim and Yaki and the others by the bog started toward him at a run.

He reached the fire before they did, sliding off into the arms of half a dozen men. By the time Rim got there, the rider was sitting on the ground. There was caked blood all over the front of his shirt and he held tightly to his left arm.

"Looks like one o' them miners from the Catalina diggin's," Lonesome said.

A skinner produced a bottle and the rider took a long, thirsty swig. Then he found his voice, speaking with hoarse effort. "Ridin' to Tucson f'r help. Damn Injuns come up on us last night. Got the whole crew pinned down in that mine."

"Apaches?" Yaki asked.

"Worse'n that. Navajos."

A dark mutter ran through the teamsters and then Lonesome asked, "Kintiel's bunch?"

"How the hell should I know?" the miner asked. "It was night when I broke through. They tried to foller but I had a fresh horse and theirs was tired."

"How many?" Yaki asked.

"Not a big party. Thirty or forty. But there's only about a dozen miners there. They don't get he'p soon, it'll be another Cerro Gordo massacre."

Yaki looked around at the men. "We

can't leave these wagons."

"What are you afraid of losing?" Rim asked pointedly.

Yaki glanced at him, eyes gleaming balefully. Then he looked down at the man on the ground. The furrows in his horsy face deepened. "All right," he said. "Lonesome, you ride to Tucson for the Army. We'll corral here. I'll leave a guard. How about a dozen volunteers?"

"Count me," Swan said.

"And me," said Rim.

That started the others and they began to assent, some with obvious reluctance. Soon Yaki had his dozen. Most of the teams had saddlers. Rim's was the off-swinger. He corralled his rig with the others and then took the animal out of its traces, getting the saddle from the wagon. Yaki left orders for those who stayed behind to finish unloading Rim's trailer and right it. The miner was in no condition to ride further and they took a Papago swamper to guide them to the Catalina. It was a new mine that had been discovered by an old desert rat just before the war. He'd sold his claim to a Tubac company and they'd sent a crew up in the fall of this year. It hadn't started to pay yet but the assay gave them high hopes. The cavalcade, most of them on saddle mules, headed eastward toward the mountains. Rim had only his Navy but the majority of the others carried Sharps buffalo guns or Yager rifles.

The desert stretched out before them, hot now under a pale sun. They passed through endless cactus flats where the pear paddles shone greasily in the shimmering light and the mules shied from the cholla spines. On the horizon palo verde was silhouetted, misty green and ghostly. The sun had dried out the greasewood and its perfume no longer hid the sour smells of sweaty leather and sweaty men.

As Rim rode, he was thinking about the sand. He tried to tell himself that this would break Romaine's operations wide open. He tried to feel justified, triumphant. Yet he had a sneaking suspicion that Romaine would squirm out of it some way, and it filled him with angry frustration. He couldn't let the man squirm out. He had to use this to pin it down for good and all.

The men rode in a subdued and watchful silence. The mules soon began to reflect their riders' tension, shying at dust devils and braying irritably when the sand clogged their nostrils. The hostility of the country was pressing in. Navajos, the miner had said. And someone had mentioned Kintiel.

Somehow, in the East, the Apaches had become symbolic of all that was bad in the Indian, a raiding, plundering tribe of killers that could not be defeated. Yet the Navajos were far worse. From their country north of the Salt they had kept the Mexicans in fear and trembling for hundreds of years. Canyon de Chelly, their legendary stronghold, had been seen by few white men, conquered by none. It stood as a symbol of their impregnability, mysterious, frightening, a little awesome. And coupled with that symbol was Hatali Kintiel.

Actually, in the Navajo language, *hatali* meant medicine man or shaman. That it should become a proper noun, used as a name, was indicative of the almost legendary status Hatali Kintiel had acquired. No white man had ever seen him. The Indians themselves talked of him with a strange mixture of hatred and awe. He was purported to have more power than any headman in the tribe, and his name seemed to hover

71

like a malignant shadow behind all the pillaging and killing and raiding that had made the territory a place of horror in the last years.

Before noon Rim began to suffer. His leg didn't bother him too much in the saddle, but the soft living of these last months had not prepared him for such a ride. His back began to ache. He grew dizzy in the heat, began to see double. His shirt was soggy with sweat, clinging like paste to his back.

Steve Swan rode up beside him, grinning at his discomfort. "No wonder they lost Bull Run. They had to depend on the likes o' you."

"Don't rub it in," Rim said. Then he looked around. They were the last in line. None of the others was paying them any attention. His thought must have shown on his face, for the one-armed Southerner chuckled ruefully.

"Where'd I go?" he said. "West you got the desert. I seen enough of it to know how quick a man who didn't know his way would git lost and die. North is the Navajos. Take more'n a one-armed Secesh t' git through them alive. East and south, it's the Apaches. Another Johnny Reb made a break that way last month. The Army found him in the Dragoons, his hair gone, his eyes pecked out by the buzzards." He looked around him at the vast and inimical desert. "No, suh, Yankee. They don't need to keep any guard on me, and they know it."

They climbed through mesquite forests where the fallen mesquite beans were inches deep on the ground, stinking with the decay of centuries. They began to pass timber, cottonwoods in the creek bottoms and ash on the slopes. In the afternoon they reached the mountains.

Here the Papago found an Indian trail leading upward. Altitude robbed the day of heat and soon the sweat was dried to a briny crust on man and beast, and the mules were coughing and groaning with the strain of climbing in the thin air. They flushed pronghorns that bounced away through the pines in fright, and squirrels chattered incessantly in the tall firs, and once far away they heard a bobcat squawl. Then they reached a fork in the trail and the Papago wanted to take the south branch.

"He's crazy," Rim said. "That won't

take you to the Catalina."

"You know where the mine is?" Yaki asked sourly.

"Not exactly. But I hunted this country with Dad. The Catalina's somewhere near Twin Saddles, and that's due north from here."

"Seems t' me an Injun'd know what he was talkin' 'bout," Yaki said. "He tells me he's packed into the mine before."

"You're working against time as it is," Rim said. "If we don't get there tonight, they might not be alive tomorrow. You want a dozen lives on your conscience?"

"I might ask you the same question."

"It's north," Rim said. "I'm going that way."

"You'll go alone then," Yaki said. "I'm takin' the Injun's word."

Yaki reined his saddler onto the south branch; with a creaking of leather, a snorting of mules, the others followed him. Swan gave Rim a rueful smile, then gigged his animal forward, followed by Calico Mills and a final rider. Rim sat his blowing animal silently, aching throughout his body from the long ride. As they passed through the shadows cast by the higher peaks and finally disappeared around a bend in the

sinuous trail, a feeling of intense loneliness and desolation swept over him.
His certainty about the location of the
mine was swept away and he had a
strong impulse to follow them. Even if
he was right, what could he do alone?
Then he swore bitterly. What the hell?

He knew he was right; he couldn't
deliberately head away from the mine.
Yet, one man riding to do battle with
forty — he felt like a fool as he wheeled
his mule and headed up the north
branch.

He was still in sight of the fork when,
glancing back, he saw a trio of riders
appear. Calico Mills and a big, crop-
headed Teuton named Tiny Anholt, and
a gaunt, consumptive old skinner they
called Lunger. Rim held his animal,
waiting for them. Sand made a grating
crunch beneath shod hoofs as they
pulled up to him. He was looking at
Calico. The man was big and potbellied,
sitting his patchwork mule in the osten-
tatious, sway-backed seat a heavy
paunch dictated. He kept pawing at the
sweat trickling down his creased, leathery neck from beneath a beard as curly
and red as mesquite grass. Its bottom
was turned black with grease from con-

stantly rubbing his filthy calico vest.

Rim was remembering the night before, on the Calle Real, and his glimpse of a calico vest on one of the fleeing men. Yet there was more than one calico vest in Tucson. And Rim had hit one of them across the face with his pistol, and there was no scar on Calico's face.

"You sure it's this way?" Calico asked.

"Dead certain," Rim said.

"I got a brother at that mine," Calico said.

Lunger coughed softly. "I don't think that Papago's packed in here. He's jist scared to come up with them Navvyho."

Rim watched Calico. "So you got a brother?"

"Sure as hell," Calico said.

Rim grinned bleakly at him; then, without a word, he turned his animal and led them on up the trail. The sun was dying and evening rushed into the canyon. Black shadows took great gulps of the distant canyons and soon only the ridges and peaks were visible. The sky turned red and then the fire burned down, leaving the reflected pink of dying coals. Purple cloud banners turned black and then the last light faded from the sky and they were riding a trail they could not see. Rim soon became so chilled that he unwrapped the blanket from behind his saddle and draped it over his coat. They picked their way slowly and silently along the trail, stopping every now and then to listen till their ears ached. Sometimes they heard an owl hoot and there were little scurryings in the brush. Then, before the moon rose, they heard the thin and brittle crack of a shot in the distance.

It echoed down rock-rimmed canyons, growing great and hollow, booming against still granite and bouncing back into spongy sandstone and finally dying in a welter of shivering sounds. They sat in tense silence long after it had died. Finally Rim spoke in a barely audible mutter.

"We better leave our mounts here. They'll probably have lookouts."

They dismounted, tethering the mules, and began to walk. Rim kept Calico on his right and ahead of him. The man was out of reach, yet Rim would know if he turned. Soon the moon rose and cast its chill light over the jagged peaks towering on every side. Another shot cracked ahead of them, closer, then a whole volley rattled against the night. By common consent the four men pulled into the cover of timber beside the trail. Moving with tense caution, they paralleled the trail as it dropped off into a canyon. In the moonlight Rim caught sight of the Twin Saddles notched deeply into the ridge of mountains on their flank.

The trail shelved down to the floor of the canyon and left the deep timber, crossing an open meadow. Beyond the meadow was more timber, silhouetted by the glow of a burning building. Standing in the black-shadowed timber, Rim said:

"They must have lookouts. If we try to cross that open ground, we'll be seen."

"What kin the four of us do?" Calico asked.

"With surprise, we might break it up," Rim said. "But we've got to nail the lookouts to surprise the main party."

"You was a captain in the war?" Lunger asked. Rim nodded. Lunger spoke again. "This the way you do it?"

"I had a company one night," Rim said. "We spread out and made 'em think we were a battalion. It put a whole regiment of Longstreet's corps on the run."

It was a damn lie, but a commission in the regulars packed authority, and they believed him.

"Whatta we do?" Anholt asked.

Rim looked up at the shoulders of the mountains. "The lookouts will be high, one side or the other. Lunger and I'll go up to the saddles. Anholt, you and Calico take this side. Try to get them without noise. Meet here as soon as you're through."

Lunger and Anholt nodded. Calico seemed to hesitate. Rim searched his bloodshot eyes for a moment. Calico finally scratched his red beard and nodded.

Rim turned with Lunger and moved across the floor of the canyon, through the aspen and the cottonwood, to the other slope. Climbing was rough going. It took the wind out of him and made his leg begin its old aching. They had to stop often, breathing heavily in the thin air, soaked with a cold sweat. The Twin Saddles were directly above them now and the timber was thinning out. They were approaching the edge of a bald meadow when they heard a horse snort.

Rim stopped, body pinned against a

fir trunk. Lunger was six feet away, blended into another tree. He pointed to their right flank. Hand tight on the butt of his Navy Colt, Rim moved in that direction. The pony stood just within the fringe of timber, stocking-footed, its rump covered with Black Arab spots. It had been cropping at the bark but now its head was high. It snorted again, whinnied. Rim halted Lunger with a signal. The man moved close to him.

"Must be an Indian horse," Rim said. "It don't like white-man smell."

Lunger looked toward the bare ridges above. "Think he heard?"

"If he has, he'll be down to see what spooked his horse," Rim said. "Why don't you circle the animal? If he shows up, he'll have to pass one of us."

Lunger nodded and moved away, muffling a cough behind his hand. Then Rim was alone. He backed away from the horse and found a thicket of underbrush. In its black shadows he settled down to wait. The horse quieted somewhat, but kept fiddling against its rope. There was no sound. The vague perfumes of the pine forest swirled about him, pungent, tantalizing. Then a little rock spilled from its bed, made a tiny clatter somewhere on the talus slope above. He had the instant impulse to move, to shift so he could see through the brush toward the sound. With a great effort he stifled it. In the freezing chill, his palm began to sweat against the revolver.

There was a long wait. The horse stirred restlessly. Rim lost any measure of time. Then sound came again.

This time it was behind him. The faintest squeak of pine needles beneath a boot. Again he had the impulse to move, to turn so that he could see. But he guessed, now, what it meant. The man could not have crossed that bare talus slope above without Rim's seeing him. He must have circled wide, then, and that first noise Rim had heard had been a rock thrown by the man from timber to draw out anybody who might be hiding in the trees. If Rim had followed his impulse, if he'd moved an inch to look, his motion would have betrayed him.

There was another squeak of needles, closer now. He did not turn his head. His breath blocked up in his throat. Sweat beaded his face and then turned cold. A shadowy flutter of movement came to his eye, ten feet away. It became the figure of a man, moving carefully from tree to tree. Rim swung his revolver till it covered the man. His Navajo was limited.

"*Taadoo nahi nani,*" he said.

The figure halted abruptly. Rim cocked his gun. The metallic click sounded startlingly loud in the silence. It telegraphed his intent better than any words could. The man knew Rim had him dead to rights, and he didn't move a muscle.

"*Bee'eldooh,*" Rim said. It was the best he could do, but the man understood. Rim saw the rifle slip from his hands and drop to the ground. Then the man spoke.

"*Haish aniti? Ha at iish biniighe yiniya?*"

It was so fast and so guttural that Rim understood none of it. He rose and stepped from the thicket. The deafening smash of the shot took him completely unaware. He heard lead whip through the thickets behind him and his whole body jerked spasmodically. At the same time he pulled his own trigger as an automatic response. But his jerk had pulled his gun aside and he missed the man. There was another crashing shot and the bullet plucked at the brim of his hat. He threw himself down, to save himself. The gun was still blasting from the downslope timber, seeking him out. He heard one bullet whack solidly into a fir above his head and a second slug kicked dirt in his face. He took a snap shot at the timber and kept on rolling. He had one glimpse of his man running for his horse in the clearing.

"Lunger!" he shouted. "Get that one with the horse."

Another shot came on the heels of his shout. He saw the cherry-red blast and stopped himself, belly down, firing deliberately at the spot. He heard a grunt of pain and a thrashing sound that ceased abruptly.

The man running for his horse reached the clearing. Lunger came into view at the same time on the other side. He shot once. The running man coughed, stumbled, and pitched onto his face. He flopped over once and then lay in a heap.

There was an abrupt stillness, like an aching pressure after those moments of deafening violence. Lunger came into the clearing and started across it toward the fallen man.

Rim called, "Watch it. There's another one."

"He took off downslope," Lunger called. "I saw him."

Rim rose and joined Lunger at the prone figure in the clearing.

"He ain't no Indian," Lunger said.

The man wore a rotten, bearskin coat, a pair of greasy rawhide britches, earth-stained Apache moccasins folded over at the knee. Rim squatted and rolled him over, face blank with surprise.

"Who is it?" Lunger asked.

"Dee Bartlett," Rim said.

"That half-breed gal's pa?"

Rim nodded, looking down into Bartlett's face. The man's eyes were open, dazed with pain and shock. He was holding his shattered arm against him.

"What're you doin' here?" Rim asked.

The man had trouble speaking. His lips barely moved. "Damn you," he said.

Rim rose. "We can't stop now. The Indians at the mine heard this. Cut his horse loose. He'll keep till we get back."

Lunger ran to the horse and chopped the rawhide rope with one swing of his skinning knife. The animal reared, wheeled, and galloped across the clearing. Rim heard Bartlett curse him, but was already heading downslope at a limping run, followed by Lunger. There was a shadowy rush of movement about the burning building in the valley below. The shots must have given the miners hope, for Rim could hear a volley from discharging rifles out of the mouths of the shafts, beyond the fire. His leg was giving him hell now and he grunted in pain every time his foot hit the ground. He passed through heavy timber, tore through underbrush, almost tripped headlong over a deadfall. Then they were on the floor of the valley, running toward the bald meadow.

Rim heard the heavy tramp of running boots ahead, and shouted, "Calico?"

"Anholt," came the answer. The huge, blond man lunged into view, running heavily through the trees, a Starr breechloader swinging at his side.

"Where's Calico?" Rim asked.

"Dunno." The man was panting heavily. "I lost him up on the mountain."

"The Indians heard our shots," Rim said. "But they know the miner that reached us got away. They'll be looking for troops from Tucson. We've got to make 'em think that's us. It's our only chance."

85

He wheeled and legged it into the shadow. He heard the two men following. Ahead, through the fringe of timber, he saw what looked like a smoky whirl of movement. As he drew closer, the fire silhouetted it, and he saw that it was the swirl of mounting men at the horse lines. He reached the other side of the meadow and plunged into the trees, opening up in the best parade-ground bawl.

"Sergeant, guide on me. Right by fours. At the gallop. Charge!"

He saw them coming at him through the trees and picked a target and fired. He missed and fired again and saw the man pitch off his horse like a sack of oats. Then Anholt and Lunger began firing and shouting too, and the echoes booming up about him sounded as deafening as a regiment.

Few of the Navajos had guns. An arrow whipped past Rim's head and buried itself in a fir. He saw the rider, a blanketed shadow on his flank, and fired, hitting the horse instead of the man. The beast reared and screamed, spilling its rider off. As the Indian rolled over, Lunger's gun smashed from behind Rim. The Indian, just coming to his feet, doubled over at the waist, coughing sickly, and fell on his face.

Dodging and running all the time, so that every shot he fired came from a different spot, Rim kept bawling the orders. "By the left of companies, forward into line, on the double, charge! Guide on me, Lieutenant. By the right flank, file left, flankers out, right by squads . . . charge!"

The words didn't matter, because the Navajos didn't understand them. But they had heard them too often before in their battles. They knew the cadence and the sound of them, and knew what they meant. And they had been primed for it. For a wild moment, Rim thought he had them convinced.

They were charging past him at a dead run, filling the night with their wild war cries and the crack of their few guns. His hammer clicked against an empty chamber. He stopped behind a tree, fumbling for his brass powder horn in the darkness. With a finger he found the empty chambers in the cylinder of his cap-and-ball and measured powder into them. Then he plucked the round lead balls from his shot pouch, seating them with the ramrod hinged under the barrel of the revolver. The crash of horses through the timber all about him and the boom of guns were deafening. A dimly seen rider hurtled past. He saw the bow raised and ducked back into timber as the string twanged. The arrow ate into ground a foot away.

He was thumbing the caps when another rush of riders surrounded him. He had but two caps on and he threw up the gun and fired almost point-blank into the face of a Navajo riding him down.

The man pitched off the rump of the horse but the animal ran against Rim, throwing him to the ground. He rolled over and fired his second shot at the last of the riders running by. He missed the man and then they were gone. But they did not go clear to the trail. He heard them hauling up in the timber, shouting at each other. The crashing of guns was gone now and there were only the sounds of running horses and calling men. Rim rolled over and rose, fumbling for more caps at the same time.

"Lunger!" he shouted. "Lunger!"

"Over here," Lunger answered, his shout half-drowned in the welter of running horses and husky voices. "I'm empty. They're all around."

"Re-form your troop," Rim bawled. "Fours right at the gallop. Sound the charge."

But it did no good now. It sounded absurd and hollow to him, like the echoes of a childish game. For too many Indians had seen him and Lunger, without catching sight of a blue uniform. Their stampede was over and they were re-forming on the high trail, jabbering excitedly and calling to those still coming from camp.

Even as he rose, Rim heard the rush of more horses bearing down on him from camp. He tried to duck back into timber and give himself time to reload. But they came out of the black-shadowed timber in a burst, moonlight fluttering across coppery bodies and flashing against lifting hoofs.

The first one was almost upon Rim before he saw him. Twisting in the saddle, he drew the string of his short war bow to his ear. Looking right down the shaft, Rim threw his useless gun in a desperate heave at the man. It struck the Indian in the face as he released the string. He was already pitching back as the arrow left his bow and it arched high in the air.

Then his horse was past and there were half a dozen behind him. Rim saw one fling up an old, brassbound pistol, another swinging a loaded short bow across his saddle. Before either could shoot there was a sudden burst of fire from the timber behind him. The man with the gun fell slantwise from his running horse and the other's arrow went wild as his pony reared in fright.

The rest of them stopped as if they had met a stone wall, their horses rearing and screaming. The fire swept out of the timber behind Rim again and he saw another man pitch out of his saddle and a pair of wounded horses crash wildly into each other, squealing in frantic pain. The remaining bucks broke and scattered at a wild gallop into timber.

It had all happened in an instant. Before Rim could recover, a rider burst from the timber behind him. He saw an old dun saddler, eyes rolling white as marbles, long ears cocked in rage. And on its back was Lonesome.

"I finally convinced Yaki you knowed what you was talkin' about," he cackled. "Looks like we made it in the nick."

Behind Lonesome rode the familiar figure of Steve Swan, a smoking revolver in his good hand. Rim grinned broadly at him, shouting hoarsely, "I never thought I'd be so glad to see a damn Johnny Reb."

Swan laughed and then threw back his head to emit an ear-splitting rebel yell. "We got 'em on the run now. Let's put the spurs to 'em."

He and Lonesome wheeled their mounts through the timber toward the sound of heavy gunfire along the trail. The crack of guns was unceasing, sending vast echoes booming back and forth down the canyon. It did sound like a regiment now. And if that weren't enough, a new volley broke out from the direction of the mine. As Rim trotted after Swan and Lonesome, he saw dismounted figures flanking him like shadows in the timber. One of them saw him and ran over. He was a huge, heavy-shouldered miner dressed in a red shirt and filthy jeans, his face blackened with powder-smoke, his eyes red-rimmed from a long night.

"Where's the Army?" he asked.

"No army. Them Indians just think there is."

"Well, damnit," the miner swore. "Here we thought we was coming out to help the Second Dragoons."

"Keep your men in a bunch," Rim said. "If you find the Indians rallying anywhere, break it up fast."

But the Indians weren't rallying. Surprised and shattered by Yaki's charge, caught between the fire of his men and the oncoming miners, the Navajos were finally convinced the Army was upon them, and were in a complete rout. Rim found Lunger and a pair of mule-skinners at the base of the trail. They told him that Yaki was chasing a bunch up the trail, and the rest had broken through and had fled singly and in little knots into the valley. Lunger was crouched over the dead body of an Indian. He was unmistakably Navajo, in his brown buckskin britches and leggings, his red, baize jacket, his belt of hand-beaten silver.

Lunger was studying the Indian carefully. "I think I seen this one before. He belongs to the Bead Clan. They're up in Canyon de Chelly with Kintiel, all right."

Lunger rose, and they were silent for a moment, with the awe that name brought. Then a man came stumbling toward them. He made a lot of noise, breaking through underbrush and cursing huskily. Rim saw that it was Calico. His side was soaked in blood and he had his left arm hugged tightly against it. Lunger went out to help him, easing the man to a sitting position against a tree. Calico's face, above his beard, was shimmering with sweat and taut with pain. Lunger squatted beside him, forcing his arm from his ribs.

"In the sidemeat," he muttered. "Must hurt like hell, but it won't kill him."

"Where'd you get it?" Rim asked.

Calico's eyes were squinted shut. "Down the valley."

"Did you?"

Calico opened his eyes, looking malevolently up at Rim. "You want me to draw a map?" he asked.

There was a raucous braying of mules and creaking of harness as the main body of skinners returned. Yaki halted his snorting saddler beside Rim, placed his ponderous, scarred hands one upon the other across the saddle horn, and leaned forward against them.

"Looks like you was right, after all," he said.

Rim's face was bleak and humorless.

"You might send one of your men up under Twin Saddles. We wounded Dee Bartlett there."

Yaki frowned. "What the hell's he doin' here?"

Rim turned to look off toward the saddles. "Maybe sellin' a little flour to the Indians."

Chapter Five

It took them a day to get Dee Bartlett and the wounded skinners back to the wagons, the best of another day to reach Tucson. News of the Navajo raid had already reached the town and a crowd gathered around the wagons as soon as they rolled into the Calle Real. Rim's outfit was one of those carrying the wounded and he halted it in the street to let the men off. A dozen willing hands helped Calico Mills and Dee Bartlett down. Bartlett's smashed arm hung in a blood-stained sling and pain made a dust-caked mask of his face.

Rim saw Corsica Bartlett pushing her way through the knots of men. She tried to take her father's good arm and support him as he moved to the doctor's house. With a feeble curse, he shook free.

"Git away from me, you damn trollop," he said.

Corsica's face turned pale and wooden with humiliation. She remained by the wagon, hands closed into fists, while Bartlett disappeared inside. Rim bent down, speaking softly.

"Why not ride into the yards with me?"

She looked up at him; her eyes were luminous with hurt. She shook her head, lips compressed, and wheeled to walk back through the crowd. The men gave way, embarrassed, unwilling to meet her eyes. Somberly Rim took up the reins.

"Haw, there. Giddap."

The Army inspected the freight that afternoon. The quartermaster and a sergeant with a squad of troopers came to the yards. They did a thorough job. They slit every bag. And they found sand every time. Then a detail rode out to arrest Harrison Day, who ran the grist mill on the Tubac road. In searching the mill, the Army came across half a dozen more bags of sand.

A hearing was held the next day. None of the army buildings was big enough to hold the score of witnesses and the audience, so they set up chairs in the Domingo Saloon. It was a dark and fetid building owned by Jacques, a mulatto who claimed origins in the island of

Santo Domingo. Major Sparks presided, a ruddy-faced veteran of Buena Vista and Monterey. He had been with the California Column when it marched from Fort Yuma to drive Sherod Hunter's Confederates out of Tucson in May of 1862.

Sparks had immediately arrested a dozen men who had given direct aid to the Confederates, sending them to the prison at Fort Yuma. But Tucson had been a hotbed of Secessionists, and it was said that, if Major Sparks had put every Southern sympathizer in Tucson under arrest, there would have been no town left.

The saloon was crowded, and Rim saw Sherry Landor seated near the front with the major's wife. All about the women sat big, sweating miners, dusty mule skinners, dark-faced Mexicans in dirty cotton clothes. Sherry kept pulling her shoulders in as they jostled her, and on her face was a look of prim disgust.

After Yaki informed the court of the details, John Romaine was called to testify. Genial, hearty, unruffled by the courtroom tension, Romaine disclaimed all responsibility. The sacks had been sealed when his wagons had taken them at the mill. There was no reason to inspect them. This was corroborated by half a dozen drivers who took the stand. The miller was then called up. Harrison Day was a ponderous, thick-witted man in his middle forties. He answered the questions slowly, thinking over each one a long time. He said he didn't know how the sacks of sand had got in his mill. He pleaded not guilty to the charges. He had no defense and no corroborating testimony.

After he stepped down, a few other witnesses were called. Rim was last. The questioning was done by Lieutenant Richard Denvers, a young shavetail, cocky and smug with his importance. Rim was able to add little to the testimony. When he was asked to step down, he turned to the major.

"Is the court satisfied with its investigation?"

Sparks looked puzzled. He toyed with a pencil on the table before him, then shrugged. "As a matter of fact, the court sees no point in continuing. It is my recommendation that the plaintiff be put under arrest and sent to Santa Fe for trial."

"Doesn't the whole thing seem a little contrived to you?"

Sparks showed his surprise. A murmur ran through the room. Sparks asked, "What do you mean, Mr. Fannin?"

"That it would take an unbelievably stupid man to commit such a crime. If we hadn't discovered the sand, it would obviously have come to light at the Papago camp and be traced back to the miller."

"Mr. Day admitted that his wife was sick and he needed money."

"There's no evidence that he got any money. He still owes his doctor bills."

"Are you saying someone else is involved?"

"I'm saying you've left too many questions unanswered. You can't possibly close the investigation at this point."

Sparks leaned forward, holding the ends of the pencil with the thumb and forefinger of each hand. "Mr. Fannin, so far you have made nothing but obscure allegations. The court would be glad to continue the investigation on the basis of new evidence. If you have any facts, will you please present them?"

Rim hesitated. His glance ran through the sea of faces to Romaine, standing by the bar. He suddenly felt hollow inside, realizing that he had no facts, only suspicion and fragments of a picture that would not come together.

"Are you basing your decision on facts?" he asked. "It's all been circumstantial evidence so far."

"Which has been enough to hang men," Sparks said. "If you have no evidence to contradict our findings, I will ask you to step down."

A rush of frustrated anger ran through Rim. "You know there's more to this than a miller stealing some corn. Ask Romaine. Why did he send twenty wagons to Sonora last week? That isn't on any regular run. Why was Dee Bartlett at the Catalina?"

Sparks stood up. "You heard his testimony. He'd just been trading with the miners."

"And the Indians too? Why should they hit the mine? They'd get a lot more out of those white settlements on the Salt. Look at the last three months. The Cerro Gordo massacre. The Copper Canyon killings. The raids that closed down the Shonto. Nothing but mines. Why?"

"Fannin, what are you trying to prove?"

"Some kind of a pattern. All these little pieces make a picture."

"What picture?"

"I don't know. But you won't even make the effort to put it together."

Sparks lost his temper. "Mr. Fannin, the Army's function is to protect this territory, not spend its time running down the unfounded suspicions of a drunken ex-soldier." He broke off, lips clamping shut over the word. Then he lowered his eyes to the desk, speaking in a stiff voice. "If you won't step down, Fannin, I will have to ask the sergeant to remove you from the room."

Trembling with anger and humiliation, Rim left the stand. He forced his way through the press of men toward the door, seeing embarrassment in some faces, derision or patronization in others. He'd been a fool. Why had he let himself go so far? As he stepped outside, moving up the street through the thinning crowd, he heard someone hurrying behind him, and turned to see Sherry.

"Rim!" She caught his arm, compassion in her face. "I'm sorry." Then she bit her lip and released his arm, her eyes dropping to the ground in embarrassment. But it had been the first impulse that counted.

"It's good to know there's still one friend left," he said.

Her eyes rose. "You wouldn't let us be friends before."

"Maybe I'm humbled now," he said. And mixed up, too. Set adrift again on the sea of confusion. Feeling like a fool again, condemning her. Maybe Sparks was right. Maybe it was all the unfounded suspicion of a drunken ex-soldier. It seemed to represent the whole trip. His reason for going now seemed shallow, illusory. Some vague wish for revenge? Some hope that he could get something on Romaine? All the intangibles rose up to gag him. His leg started throbbing dully again.

Sherry tucked a hand into his arm. "Walk me home."

Before they could start, Romaine and Yaki issued from the door. Romaine removed his hat and tilted his massive head gallantly.

"You should walk about more, Sherry. This barren land needs such a breath of beauty."

She could not hide her pleasure. "Thank you, John."

Romaine put his flat-topped hat back on his head, looking with veiled eyes at Rim. "You said there were many questions unanswered." He touched a luxuriant burnside almost reverently. "What were they?"

Bleak hollows formed under Rim's sharp cheekbones. "Why didn't you want me on that trip, for instance?"

Romaine produced a cigar, inclined his head toward Sherry. "Your permission?" Sherry nodded. Romaine got out his penknife and carefully pared off the cigar end, studying it with pursed lips. "Why should I hire a man who'd like nothing better than to see my ruin?"

"Then why did you hire me?"

"It's my policy to accede to my wagon boss in matters of the trail." Romaine clamped the cigar between strong, white teeth. With his lips pulled back, he looked as though he were grinning. But he wasn't. He spoke that way, around the cigar. "However, Yaki tells me of your failure at the bog. He was very disappointed. It's unlikely he'll hire you again."

He took out his huge gold watch,

snapping it open. Then he removed the cigar from between his teeth, inclining his head toward Sherry. "You'll excuse me. Appointment."

He shouldered through the crowd, a big, broad man in his impeccably tailored scissortail, emanating power and influence. In a few seconds he was surrounded by half a dozen men. Major Sparks joined him and Romaine threw an arm over his shoulder, saying something, and Sparks threw back his head to laugh. Yaki Peters watched this; then turned an enigmatic look to Rim.

"I guess I'll be goin'," he said. "That sounded like a prime joke."

As the wagon boss shambled after Romaine, Sherry tucked her hand in Rim's elbow again. "You were going to walk me home."

Anger dying in him, he accompanied her moodily down the street. "I expected to see your uncle at the hearing."

"He's out contracting with the Santa Cruz mill for another load of flour," she said. He walked silently beside her and finally she spoke again. "You're still brooding about Romaine. What could he have gained out of this?"

"A small fortune," Rim said. "Out at

the mines a bag of flour brings three or four times what a government contract pays. There were five hundred bags in that load."

"But the miller. . . ."

"He couldn't have shipped it. Romaine's the only one in the territory with enough wagons for such an operation."

"He wouldn't be that foolish," she said. "He'd be cutting his own throat."

Rim knew what she meant. The Apaches had gone on the warpath over a violated treaty; the trouble in the last year had pushed the Pimas almost to the same point. No telling their reaction if the sand had reached their villages. The freighting business was precarious enough, without another tribe added to the warring Navajos and Apaches.

They had reached the Landor house and Sherry invited him into the parlor. This was Sherry's room, a place of milk-white Sandwich lamps and Boston rockers, spool-turned settees and tabernacle mirrors. The clawed feet of the chairs clutched impotently at the hard-packed mud floor; the carving on the japanned dressing table insulated the peasant simplicity of whitewashed mud walls. Nowhere was the barbaric splendor of a Navajo blanket or the crude strength of the hand-carved furniture usually adorning one of these Tucson houses. This was a corner of civilization transported to the wilds, a sanctuary of peace and gentility in a wasteland of savagery. And to him it was a room stiff and dreary and almost frightening in its effort to remain aloof from the country and the people around it.

He sat down on the striped damask of a chair and felt uncomfortable. There was a copy of the *New York Tribune* on the table.

"They print a paper in Santa Fe too," he said.

She ignored it. "We just got some wonderful blueberry wine," she said.

"No plain old *mula blanca?*"

She poured the wine and brought it to him. "Rim," she said, "don't mock me."

He shook his head. "I'm sorry. I just thought you'd get over it eventually."

She sat down, her hands folded. There was something intensely prim and New England about her now. She studied the hooked rugs on the floor.

"I've tried," she said. "You know I have."

"It's not such a bad place. A lot of

women have got used to it."

"To what?" she said. "The sand blowing all the time? The mud in winter, the heat in summer? It will be summer again soon, Rim. Like walking into a furnace. I dread it." She rose restlessly, walked to a window. "I went to the edge of town today. Looking out at that desert. Does it ever end?"

"Somewhere."

"And the people, Rim. You seem so at home with them."

"You have to speak their language, Sherry."

"I've tried to learn Spanish."

"I don't mean just the words."

She was silent. He studied the stiff line of her back. This had stood between them before, though not so strongly. All the bitterness of the war seemed to have been brought to a head. He could understand it, in a way. She had led a sheltered life, till her uncle brought her west. The crudity and brutality of the frontier had shocked her; the savagery and cruelty of the land itself had made her withdraw. But beneath her gentility, her sensitivity, Rim had seen a strength that he had hoped would allow her to adjust to this barbaric new world.

He had tried to show her the beauty of the land and the people, as he saw them. Somehow he had failed.

The blueberry wine tasted sweet and pallid beside the raw fire of the Mexican drinks he was used to. He set it down. She turned.

"You don't like it."

"I do," he lied. He stood up. "There's enough of a gap between our two worlds now, Sherry. Don't keep putting up more walls."

"What about the walls you put up?" she said. "This Romaine thing's becoming an obsession."

He shook his head. "There are so many things I can't forget. You heard my testimony about what happened up at the Catalina. When I stepped out to get Dee Bartlett, somebody tried to kill me."

"Obviously the Navajo lookout you never found."

"Why obviously? I shot back. I drew blood. And half an hour later, Calico Mills stumbled in with a bullet through his short ribs."

"A lot of skinners got hit in the fight." She clasped her hands, trying to keep annoyance from becoming anger.

"You're making something out of nothing."

"Am I? Only four men knew about the sand at that time. Yaki is Romaine's man. Lonesome sold out a long time ago. That Johnny Reb would keep his mouth shut if it meant his neck. Which only leaves me."

She said impatiently, "Didn't the whole town know about the sand the minute you got back?"

"After somebody had failed to kill me at the Catalina," he said.

"Rim, you're being fantastic again. I'm so tired of your ugly suspicions. So tired of these constant arguments."

He went toward her in an anger of his own. "Maybe I am too, Sherry. I think these fights about Romaine only cover something deeper. We had something before the war. Why can't we get it back?"

It was the nearest they had been, face to face, in a long time. He could see it bring a breathlessness to her. A flush came to her pale cheeks. This was a hint of the passion and need that had always lain so tantalizingly beneath the restrained surface of her. He was filled with a burning urge to touch it again, as he had before, to draw it out of her, fully and finally.

He took her in his arms and pulled her against him. The instant heat and softness of her seemed to burn like a fire. For a moment her lips were moist and giving against his. The whole length of her quivered in his arms.

Then the fire went out. Her body grew rigid. Her lips became tight and unyielding. It was like kissing a marble statue.

He let her go, and she stepped back. Her face was taut, her eyes wide. He saw the years of inhibition and sheltered prudery welling up in those eyes, rejecting him, preventing her from giving vent to the animal needs of her body. This was what he fought, beneath the smoke screen of their arguments over Romaine. This was the core of the wall between them. Before the war he had hoped to break through that wall. Now he saw how futile the hope had been. To her he was a part of this country — the savagery, the violence, the primitive passions that she hated. She had tried to bridge the gap herself. There had been a need in her, a reaching out to him. But every time he tried to answer, she withdrew. She was helpless before a lifetime of conditioning.

"Is it always going to be tea and cakes and blueberry wine and napkins on the knees?"

"Rim!" Her eyes were tortured.

He felt his shoulders sag. It had only been the gnawing sense of defeat speaking, the last striking out at an enemy he could not bring down. "Never mind," he said. "You're right. The sand does blow all the time. And it's hot as hell in the summer."

Chapter Six

The Domingo Saloon stood just beyond the Callejon del Herrero, on the main street of town. Its central room was a dark and sinister chamber, low-ceilinged, floored with sawdust. There was a fine, walnut bar shipped in from St. Louis before the war, over which hung a gaudy oil painting of a fleshy nude. Beneath this stood the dozen heavy bar barrels in their racks, so evenly balanced that a child could pour a drink from a fifty-gallon keg. The painting and the barrels were Jacques's pride and joy, and it was said that he had murdered one of Sherod Hunter's Confederates for shooting a hole in the end keg.

The publicity of the hearing earlier in the day had left the saloon more crowded than usual. The bar was lined with troopers and freighters and miners, and there was a sweating knot of kibitzers around all the short card tables. Rim saw Tiny Anholt and Lunger playing freeze-out with Portigee Phillips, another White Mountain teamster. At the far end of the room, Steve Swan and Lonesome were drinking with other Romaine men. Rim shouldered his way through the boisterous crowd. The need for a drink was gnawing at him. What the hell? More than one drink. He wanted to throw a whing-ding. He wanted to forget Sherry and his defeat this afternoon and all his gathered bitterness in a wild, roaring drunk.

How often before had Sherry's rejection of him driven him here these last months? He didn't want to count. There seemed no goals left in life, nothing to cling to. He saw Jacques sitting at a wall table with Sergeant Patrick Briggs, the biggest drunk in the Second Dragoons. Jacques hailed him.

"Ah, my fran', you are jus' in time to make wassail over Briggs's removal from incarceration. A month in the guardhouse he get for his las' drunk here, and now he comes back to do it all over again."

Briggs's laugh was raucous as a mule bray. Rim sprawled into an empty chair, moodily taking the glass of mescal Jacques poured him. The mulatto was a broad, potbellied man with a fat moon of a face, its crevices always greasy with sweat. Somewhere he had lost his left hand; in its place was a silver doorknob socketed to the stump of his wrist with leather. He had a row of empty glasses of varying sizes before him, and played a tune on them with the knob as he talked.

"You see Archuleta?"

Rim nodded, tossing off the mescal neat.

"He the one who tell you about them twenty wagons they go south?"

Rim nodded again, squinting watery eyes.

"What you think?"

Rim said, "I think Romaine put sand in the government shipment and sent the real flour to the Sonora mines. He can get four times the price down there."

"Perhaps you are right." Jacques played "Boots and Saddles" with his silver knob. Then he sighed. "You look so depress' again, my fran'. To the house of that foolish woman you have been."

Sergeant Briggs leaned forward. He had beefy shoulders and a rugged face, its leathery furrows burned brick red by the sun and always stubbled with a day's growth of beard. "It ain't the gal plaguin' him," he said. "It's the goddamn Army. They ain't got the sense t'see the nose on their face."

Rim looked into his bloodshot eyes. "Don't bait me."

"I'm not kiddin'," Briggs said. "I was on the detail that searched the mill. That miller might be thick-headed, but he ain't dumb enough to leave six sacks of sand around where anybody kin find 'em."

Rim looked into their drunken, sweating faces. It helped to have someone believe in him. The irony of it struck him again. Was this the only place in town he could gain acceptance? This den of thieves and drunks and outcasts? Jacques poured him a second drink and he emptied it. Briggs launched into one of his obscene jokes and they all began laughing drunkenly.

Then Corsica was there. Rim hadn't seen her enter but she was suddenly in front of him. He grabbed her arm and pulled her onto his lap. She smelled of powder and cheap perfume. The softness she showed him when they were alone was gone from her face. It bore the mechanical smile that was stock in trade of so many women from the Callejon. She pressed her ripeness against him and ran her fingers through his hair.

"Reem, com' with me. . . ."

"Why?" He was drunk and he knew it. Pretty soon he wouldn't even know it any more. "Have a drink. We're here to forget, Corsica. Forgive and forget."

"Com' with me." Her voice was insistent. There was something frightened behind the fixed smile. It brought a teasing memory to him. Something about the wagon yards. She had tried to warn him then.

"Corsica," he said, "why didn't you want me to go with the wagon train?"

Her eyes darted around the room. "I no can tell you here."

"Was it the sand? Did you know the sand was in those bags?"

"Please, Reem."

Briggs smote the table again, shouting drunkenly. "Can't you see she wants you alone, boy? Don't keep the lady waiting."

Rim took another drink. His vision blurred. "Or maybe it was the Indians." He sought to retain the thought. "The

116

Indians," he repeated solemnly. His head jerked back, blinking his eyes at her. "Your dad was up there at the Catalina. Was that it? Did you know about the Indians?"

She shook her head, more in angry helplessness than in denial. She slid off onto her feet, trying to pull him from his chair. Her shoulder-length hair had fallen across one side of her face, black, silken, tantalizing. He pulled her to his lap again, caught her soft, oval face in both hands, and pulled it down to him. Both Briggs and Jacques set up a great, roaring shout. But he paid them no heed. In a drunken and savage reaction against all the frustration and rejection Sherry had given him, he kissed her. He kissed her hard and long, bruising her lips, drawing a soft moan of mingled pleasure and pain from her, taking all she had to give, holding her yielding body against his till its softness and its heat ran through him like a fever.

"Petite drôlesse du diable!" Jacques shouted. "This kiss I should pickle in a bottle and put on the bar for all to marvel at."

"Reem," she whispered. "Please . . . not here."

117

He wanted to go with her now. He let her slide off his lap again. She held his hands to pull him up. Before he came off the chair, there was a crack like a gunshot. A long black snake of a thing came whirling out of nowhere and wrapped itself around Corsica's waist. She cried out sharply in pain. Then she was jerked off her feet and thrown heavily on the floor. From somewhere in a vast distance, Rim heard the roaring voice.

"I told you what I'd do the next time I caught you honey-suckin' aroun' with these yere pike-country coons!"

Rim finally got his eyes focused on the source of the shout. It was Yaki Peters, standing fifteen feet away, holding the stock of his mule whip high. Its other end was still wrapped around Corsica, who had been thrown to the floor. Rim came out of his chair on wobbly legs.

"Yaki . . . let 'er go."

Corsica tried to rise. Yaki gave a jerk on the whip, spilling her flat again. "I'm agoin' t' teach this one a lesson," he bawled.

Rim threw his chair at the man. Yaki didn't duck soon enough and it slammed him back against the bar, tearing the whip from his hand. With a curse and a shake of his head, he charged across the room. Rim kicked another chair into his path and Yaki sprawled over it and went flat on his face, fingers clawing the toes of Rim's boots.

The place exploded into an immediate uproar. On every side drunken men, eager for a fight, were jumping up from their chairs. With a happy roar, Briggs climbed on top of his table and threw himself bodily into a gang of White Mountain teamsters. Portigee Phillips pulled his knife and started slashing wildly. Rim was caught from behind, whirled around, and smashed in the face by Tiny Anholt.

It knocked him ten feet backward. Only the bar kept him from falling. Elbows hooked over its top, he hung against the walnut, dazed and helpless for a moment. He had a blurred vision of Anholt rushing him to finish the job. Then one of Briggs's wild blows knocked Steve Swan between Anholt and Rim. Anholt tripped and both of them tumbled to the floor at Rim's feet.

With a Teutonic oath, Anholt grabbed the bar and heaved himself up. Swan clawed at the man's legs. It wasn't apparent whether he was trying to stop Anholt or just get to his feet. Anholt shifted his weight to stamp the Southerner's face in.

Still dazed, Rim threw himself at Anholt's legs. He knocked the man backward and Anholt pitched full to the floor, driven flat by Rim's weight. His head hit the cement-hard adobe and his whole body went limp beneath Rim. As Rim got to his hands and knees, he saw Swan pulling himself erect, a reckless grin on his face.

"Thanks, Yank. Them Cha'lston gals wouldn't like me with a flat face."

Rim had no time to react. Before he was fully on his feet, Portigee Phillips reeled into him. The pock-marked man slashed wildly with his knife and Rim threw up an arm to block it. That left him open across the belly and Portigee drew back for a vicious thrust there. He saw the knife coming and couldn't drop his arm in time. He had a moment of pure animal fear.

Then a bottle crashed across Portigee's head and the man fell against Rim without completing his thrust. He slid down Rim's legs with blood flowing in a sheet down his stunned face and Rim saw Steve Swan standing behind the man, the broken neck of the bottle in one hand.

"One for one," the rebel grinned. "Now, we're even." He swung the bottle at Rim. Rim ducked and it smashed against the bar. He saw Swan's face in front of him and struck at it and Swan went over backward. The whole place was rocking with the frenzied mob of kicking, brawling, clubbing men now. Jacques had jumped atop the bar and was running up and down in front of his prized painting, using a bung starter on anybody foolish enough to get within ten feet of it.

Rim had no coherent sense of the rest of the brawl. He only knew it was a wild release of the pent-up frustration and bitterness of the past weeks, and he entered into it with all the drunken eagerness of Briggs. He smashed faces and got smashed back; he kicked and clawed and shouted; he broke chairs over heads and got thrown onto a table and smashed it to bits; he got rolled on the floor and got kicked into a stupor of dazed pain. Then Briggs lifted him to his feet again and he forgot it in a few moments, standing back to back with the man and flailing at everyone who came into range.

After a while, they found themselves outside. Rim was sitting against the wall, his face smeared with blood, his head spinning. Men kept stumbling out of the saloon, wiping blood from their faces. Two miners who had been slugging at each other ten minutes before were walking up and down the Calle Real arm in arm, singing an obscene song. Briggs leaned against one of the poles supporting the thatched overhang, spitting out teeth and blood.

"I think I'm sober again, dammit."

Steve Swan weaved out, sought support against a wall. One side of his jaw was swollen the size of an orange. He rubbed it in drunken meditation.

"Yank, if you can fight like that, how in hell did you lose Bull Run?"

Rim was beginning to feel the aftereffects now. His whole body throbbed and ached. He tried to gain his feet, wincing and grimacing. He heard hoofbeats in the darkness and a horse snorted. A detail of cavalry came out of the night. Light from the Domingo winked against brass buttons and accouterments. The horsemen stopped and Rim saw that there were three troopers and the young shavetail who had done the questioning at the hearing — Lieutenant Denvers, his pink cheeks raw and rough now from desert winds, his uniform grayed by dust.

"What's this, Sergeant?" he asked.

Briggs assayed a sloppy salute, trying to hide his puffy eye. "I lost me collar button, Lootenant. Huntin' around on the ground I was, come up ag'in Mr. Fannin's boot I did, tripped him up so that he fell on his face and made all that bloody mess, raised a mouse on me own eye. The Johnny Reb was jist comin' out the door as I lifted up, an' the top o' me skull struck his jaw."

"That's enough, Briggs. Report directly back to the guardhouse. You'll be lucky to keep your stripes this time."

Briggs looked sadly at his stripes. "A sad world it is whin a man loses his stripes and his collar button all in the same night."

There was a fifth horse between two of the troopers. At first Rim thought it was a pack horse. But slowly the outline of its load became definable to him — a man slung across the saddle, head

123

dangling on one side, feet on the other. Rim walked out to the animal. The dead man was Wylie Landor.

The shock of it took the last of the drink from Rim. Feeling sick, he looked at Denvers. The Lieutenant's face was sober and grim.

"We were on patrol," he said. "Found him east of the Tubac road."

They had wrapped Landor's coat around his head. It was soaked with blood. Rim stepped back a little, his face gray, his stomach churning. Others were gathering now. Yaki Peters shambled from the saloon, coiling his whip. The rancid look he sent Rim faded as he saw the corpse. Corsica followed him, sliding immediately to one side along the wall, till she stood a safe distance from Yaki. She was looking at the body all the time, eyes wide and luminous in a taut face.

Denvers leaned out of his saddle, handing Rim a scrap of paper. "We found this under his body. Apparently he wasn't dead when they scalped him. Lived long enough after they left to start it."

Rim saw that it was an invoice from White Mountain. The writing was in pencil — Wylie would always have his pencil — and it was scrawled on the blank side of the paper. Just five words:

Rim was right. Try to. . . .

After that, nothing, save a smear of blood.

"What could it mean?" the lieutenant asked.

Rim looked up at him in bleak anger. "You were at that hearing."

"You were right about what?" Denvers said. "You were flinging so many wild ideas around."

"Maybe about Romaine," Rim said.

"Or Bartlett, or the flour, or the Indians. It could mean anything," Denvers said. He held out his hand. "I'll have to turn it over to the major."

Rim handed the scrap of paper back, glancing at the dead man. "Don't let his niece see him like this."

The lieutenant nodded. "Perhaps you'd better be the one to tell her, Fannin. You were a close friend."

Rim nodded. He knew a deep reluctance. But someone had to tell Sherry, and he hated to think of a comparative stranger doing it. His coat was torn to

125

ribbons and he stopped at his place to clean up. Then he went to Sherry's house. It was after eleven but there was a light in the parlor. Apparently she was waiting up for her uncle. She met him at the door, the back-light turning her sun-mist hair to a golden corona. At the sight of his cut, bruised face, her lips compressed.

"If you're drunk," she said, "I'd rather not see you, Rim."

"I'm not drunk, Sherry. Let me come in. I've got something to tell you."

The grim look of him made her step back, and he entered. He paced the room a moment, hunting for words. He had the wish to prepare her somehow. But any preface seemed hollow, and she would sense what he meant before he finished. Finally he told her simply, briefly, the best way in the end.

He saw the shock hit her, and was afraid. Her hands bunched up in the hoop skirt till the cloth tore; her face went chalk white, turning loose and wild. For a moment he thought she would go to pieces. Then she swayed, her eyes losing focus, and he went swiftly to her and took her in his arms. She leaned heavily against him. Her

126

fingers began digging into his arms, fiercely, and she buried her face against his chest. Sobs shook her body. He held her tightly for a long time and finally the spasms quieted.

She pulled back, disengaging herself. She walked carefully to the spool-turned settee and sat down. Little muscles twitched in her mouth. Her eyes were squinted shut and her hands were locked in her lap. She was fighting for control. This was the strength and the courage and the vitality he had always seen beneath her prudery, her withdrawal. He went to her again and knelt before her, covering her hands with his.

"Sherry, if there's anything in the world I can do, you know I will. . . ."

She nodded. "It's all right now," she said. Her voice was small, tight. "I think it's over."

He went to the highboy for some of Landor's Scotch and poured her a stiff drink. She didn't want it, but he made her take it. It brought a little color back to her face. Then he put the coffeepot on. While he was at it, Major Sparks and Dr. Crain arrived. The doctor had been Landor's close friend. He took Sherry into the bedroom and made her lie down. Rim poured Sparks a cup of coffee. The major took it, shaking his head.

"A bad thing," he said. "A bad thing."

The doctor came out after a while. "I've given her an opiate," he said. "It will help her to sleep. It's been a terrible shock to her."

Major Sparks left in a few minutes. The doctor and Rim remained. They had made another pot of coffee and talked about Landor and a lot of other things. Neither of them felt like sleeping and finally they settled down to a game of stud.

Sherry woke shortly after dawn. Her face looked pale, drawn, but she was calm. Rim cooked breakfast and Crain made her eat something. Toying with the eggs, she said: "They say there's a wagon train going to Santa Fe next week."

Rim looked sharply at her, but she would not raise her eyes from her plate. This was what he had expected and feared from the first moment he had seen Landor's body. Her uncle's death was the final justification of her hatred of this land. Finally, with the weight of Rim's attention bearing against her, she raised her eyes, almost defensively.

"I have people in New Hampshire," she said. "I never should have come out here. I did it for Uncle Wylie. He thought it would be better, after Dad's death. I should have stayed back there. I *never* should have come." She shook her head and looked emptily at the wall. "There's nothing to hold me here now."

Rim's broad shoulders bowed. "No," he admitted, "I suppose there isn't."

Chapter Seven

Thirty wagons were going north, under
the escort of two troops of cavalry.
Though Major Sparks had not made
their load and destination public, it
could hardly be kept secret in a town
such as Tucson. It was known that the
train would be carrying a prize that had
passed back and forth between Confederates and Unionists several times in
the first year of the war — the arms and
ammunition that Rim Fannin's father
had tried to run to Fort Yuma. Sherod
Hunter, after killing Sean Fannin and
capturing the load, had returned to
Tucson. Later, forced to retreat eastward by the arrival of the California
volunteers, Hunter had tried to take the
guns with him. But an advance troop
of Union cavalry had cut off the supply
train and recaptured the arms.

Two days after Landor's death, a pri-
vate found Rim in town and told him
Major Sparks would like to see him.
They rode to the barracks and found

Sparks in the squalid mud shack that sufficed for his quarters and office. With him was John Romaine.

Seeing the stiff expression come to Rim's face, Sparks rose from behind the rickety table he used for a desk and waved a hand impatiently at both of them.

"Let's try to subordinate personalities to the good of the country, Fannin. I feel that basically all your trouble these last months has come from a sincere patriotism, however misplaced it may be."

Romaine touched a burnside; toyed with his heavy watch chain; smiled blandly. Rim had a bad taste in his mouth. He shook his head tiredly.

"All right. What are you leading up to?"

Sparks picked up a pencil. "I suppose you've guessed what the wagons are carrying?"

"Who hasn't? According to the word at the Domingo, you're sending the guns to Fort Defiance."

Sparks nodded, twirling the pencil. "As you know, Colonel Kit Carson has started a campaign against the Navajos. This time it won't be over till they're completely broken. Carson has some regulars, but he's using a lot of volunteers, too. That means that they'll need arms. The department probably had this in mind when they commanded me to hold those Harper's Ferries here till further orders. At any rate, they're on the way to Fort Defiance now, and we need another driver."

Rim looked at Romaine. The man turned away and walked to a window, thumbing his watch chain. Sparks shrugged.

"Romaine didn't want you to go. We've convinced him it would be dangerous to hire an inexperienced man. An hour lost over a hot box might be just the thing to put a war party in their laps."

Rim looked at Romaine's broad back. What was in the man's mind? The job would take Rim out of Tucson for months. Yet Romaine hadn't wanted to hire him. The man hadn't wanted to hire him before either, and he'd found the sand. Was that the key? Was something going to happen on this trip that Romaine didn't want Rim in on?

"What are you going to do about Wylie Landor?" Rim asked.

The major shook his head. "Isn't that beside the point?" .

"Not at all. You saw that paper they found on him. He knew something, Major. You can't just close the books on it."

"All right. If you must know, we're investigating. We're doing everything we can to find out how and why he was murdered. We haven't released Dee Bartlett from custody yet and we're looking deeper into this episode of the sand in the flour bags. Does that satisfy you?"

Rim looked at Romaine again. Sparks shook his head angrily. "Romaine's clear, Fannin. You don't think I'd let a man handle the shipping for my entire command before I checked him thoroughly, do you? Now I've done all I can. I've admitted what you said at the hearing might have some foundation in fact. Something's going on and we're trying to get to the bottom of it. Cleaning out the Navajos will help. And getting those guns to Defiance is a big part of it. How about your answer?"

Romaine had turned. His eyes were muddy with rancor and he made no attempt to maintain his mask of geniality. But Rim was considering the other things now. In a way, he owed this to his dad. Sean Fannin had given his life over those guns, and this would be sort of finishing the job for him. There was Sherry, too. Rim hadn't been able to get through to her since Landor's death. He knew it was the shock. Perhaps, by the time they reached Fort Defiance, that shock would be gone. Perhaps he could make her see. . . .

"I'll go," he said.

He went to his house for his gear, his whip, his arms. Then he walked to the White Mountain yards. The thirty wagons and their trailers jammed the flats from buildings to corrals. It was the usual insanity of braying mules, cursing skinners, sweating swampers. A detail of troopers from the barracks was helping load, presided over by Lieutenant Denvers. He was everywhere on his dancing bay, berating the grumbling troopers by book and page.

Denvers saw Rim looking at the crates being hoisted into the dusty beds of the Murphys. "Harper's Ferry, fifty-five," he called through the haze of dust. "Get any of those, Mr. Fannin."

Rim grimaced. He knew the gun. Maynard primer and rifle barrel, five hundred grains of bullet and sixty of powder. Ten shots in a four-inch group at a hundred yards if you were a sharpshooter, anybody's guess if you weren't. A few freaks coated with something brown that the contractor called varnish. One-fifth ounce dragon's oil, one ounce shellac, dissolved in one quart of alcohol. That's what the specifications said, anyway. But the stink it made when the gun heated up caused the troopers to ascribe a name other than varnish to it, and ingredients other than dragon's oil.

Rim found Yaki Peters in the usual lather of last-minute loading. The man could spare but one sour look and a wave of his great, scarred hand, with its two stiff fingers.

"Number Thirty, across the yard by the corrals."

The last in line again. Eating the dust and tramping the droppings, the last to pull out in the morning, the last to pull in at night. Rim wondered if Yaki had done it on purpose.

Two sweat-soaked troopers were helping Papago swampers load the wagon with crated guns. Rim threw his gear up onto the seat. There was no team and he spent a wild half hour finding harnesses and getting the mules into them. Then he ran the team through

135

the heehawing madness of the yard and got it backed into the tongue.

He was unsnarling the jerk line when he heard the tinkling. At first he thought it was somebody's trace chains. Yet it was different, somehow, a brittle, little clash of metal that would not stop, like the bells on a moving outfit. And no outfit was moving.

Somehow it was reminiscent of another night, another tinkling. Looking around for its source, he suddenly caught sight of the woman. She stood fifty feet away, near the tail of another outfit. She was Navajo, dressed in a vest of blue velvet. Her skirt was made from the wool of a red bayeta blanket, full about her coppery calves, held tightly about her slim waist by a turquoise belt. There was something completely primitive about her in that moment; her utter stillness seemed to partake of the earth and the wind and the sky, of things a white man could never know. For an instant it was like a spell. Rim could not hear the uproar about him. They were alone in a new world, staring at each other.

Then he heard the tinkling again. It wasn't the rattle of her jewelry, for she

136

was still motionless. He realized that he was stiffening like a dog at an unseen threat. Then, like a shadow, a man joined her.

He seemed to come from behind the wagon, though Rim could not be sure. He had a narrow, hatchet-shaped face, bead-blank eyes, an insolent swagger. He wore the traditional red wool jacket and rawhide leggings buttoned at the knees. He affected a prodigious amount of silver jewelry. Earrings and necklaces, bracelets and belts, a hundred pendants dangling from the brim of his Mexican sombrero — all of silver. His slightest motion brought the barbaric clash of those bracelets, the eerie tinkle of those pendants.

And Rim knew what the sound had nudged in his memory. It was the same sound he had heard that night in town after leaving Archuleta, when he'd seen the Indian following him; the same sound he'd heard when the pair of men attacked him, and Steve Swan had run them off with the whip. He looked for a scar on the Indian's face that might have been made by his pistol barrel. There was none.

As Rim stood gazing at them, a trooper joined him. It was Sergeant Briggs, scrubbing sweat from inside his collar and muttering Gaelic oaths.

"Don't tell me you're with us," Rim said.

"I had me choice. Three months in the guardhouse or a tour on this divil's journey. I must be goin' soft in the head."

Rim nodded at the Indians. "Who are they?"

"Belong to a clan of Navajos Denvers picked up near the Gila. They might be friendly, but Sparks ain't takin' a chance. Carson's rounding up the whole tribe. We're supposed to herd this bunch to Defiance for him."

"I never saw so much jewelry."

"Them Navajo men wear more'n the women, I swear. This boy's name is Peshlikai. Means the Silversmith, or somethin'."

More Navajos had appeared behind the young woman and man; a grizzled old headman, a pair of younger men, half a dozen murmuring women. They were under the guard of a pair of troopers, who halted them, apparently waiting for Briggs. The sergeant cursed again, and went toward them.

"All right," he growled. "Let's go. On the double."

The young man made an insolent gesture with one hand that started his silver jangling again; then he turned and joined the others. The woman went after him. Just before she disappeared, she turned and looked once more at Rim.

They left Tucson with the first heat of the sun scorching the ancient buildings. They wheeled out of the White Mountain yards under the escort of two troops of the Second Dragoons, commanded by Lieutenant Denvers. One groaning wagon after another, with the great wheels creaking and the mules braying and the curses echoing flatly against blank adobe walls, they grumbled and rattled and clanked down Royal Street and through the gap in the old wall, waking stray dogs and scattering Mexicans and Indians who were sitting sleepily against the buildings. The dust was like a chalky haze in the air about them and the Catalinas were a sleeping vapor on the horizon, gaining folds and spines and ridges as the unraveling miles brought them closer.

In the hectic moments of leaving, Rim had missed Sherry's arrival, and did not know that she was riding in Lonesome's wagon, directly ahead of him, till after they left the town. He wanted to go up and talk with her, but he remembered the last time he had let his attention be diverted from his wagon. So he contented himself with slouching on the high seat beside his swamper, Jonathan Street, while they passed at a snail's pace through the endless pear flats and the flat, sandy bottoms of the Santa Cruz.

At the night halt, Rim corralled his wagon and walked up to Lonesome's rig. Sherry was about to climb down and he held up a hand. For a moment, as she swung off, her weight came against him, a tantalizing hint of silk and flesh, and the scent of lilacs filled the air. Then she moved back, looking gravely into his face.

"That grub line's pretty rough," he said. "I thought maybe you'd like me to fetch your sowbelly and biscuits."

"Thank you, Rim," she said.

He shouldered his way into the line of teamsters formed at the Dutch ovens. But when he got back to Lonesome's rig with the loaded plates, he found Steve Swan there. Sherry was seated on a crate, a plate already in her lap. She looked helplessly at Rim.

"I'm sorry," she said. "I told him I already had an offer."

"Looks like Yankee ingenuity has to bow to Southern gallantry again," Swan grinned.

Rim set down the plates, scowling fiercely. "Your parole is revoked. Report back to the guardhouse."

Swan laughed heartily. Rim saw that it even brought a faint smile to Sherry's lips. But it died almost immediately.

"Miss Sherry tells me you blame her for leaving this Godforsaken country," Swan said.

Rim glanced at Sherry. She would not look up from her plate. "Blame is hardly the word," Rim said. "I just think she hasn't given it a chance."

"A chance?" Sherry's voice was brittle. "How much more can I give it? When it's taken everything dear to me . . ." she broke off, lips compressed. Then, with an effort, "I'm sorry. Let's not talk about it."

"I think you're right," Swan said. "This is no land for a lady. You should come

141

to Virginia, ma'am. You were meant for a country like that. Grace and beauty and charm. . . ."

Rim saw Sherry react to that. A faint flush tinted her cheeks. The Southerner knew where to touch her. And this land didn't. And he was a part of this land. A restlessness ran through him and he rose with his half-empty plate. What a fool he'd been to think he could accomplish anything with Sherry on this trip! Her mind was made up. It had been made up from the first moment she had set foot in New Mexico territory.

He finished his meal by his wagon and washed the plate and cup with sand and ashes, stuffing them into his war sack with his other gear. He pulled his blanket roll from behind the seat and turned to throw it under the bed of the wagon. Not ten feet away a figure was passing. He saw that it was the Indian woman. She had been to the river for a pail of water. She stopped.

They were in semi-darkness here, out of the circle of light cast by the flickering fire. He had but a dim impression of her, eyes that seemed too big for her shadowy cameo of a face, willow-slim body, surprisingly ripe lips, red as candlewood blossoms. Her hair was not bound into the traditional squash blossoms at the side of her head now. She had taken it down, and it fell below her waist, glossy-black as a wet beaver pelt. The silence grew awkward, and he tried his meager Navajo.

"*Nishtli* Rim Fannin," he said. "I am Rim Fannin."

She did not answer.

"*Haash yinilghe?*" he said. "What is your name?"

Still she did not answer. The words seemed to make no impression on her. There was something eerie about her total silence. There were little hollows at her temples and beneath her exotic cheekbones, stained with shadows, tawny as gold. Her grave, wide-eyed regard made him nervous, and he started to try again. Before he could speak, however, he heard the muted jangle of silver.

The Indians were seated in a blanketed circle beside the wagon in which they were riding, three outfits away. From this shadowy group one figure had risen and was walking toward Rim. It was Peshlikai, the silversmith.

He stopped beside the woman and

said something to her in quick, guttural Navajo that Rim could not understand. Without looking at Peshlikai, she turned and walked back to her people. Even in movement she made no sound.

Rim was tired of the failure of his limited Navajo. These people had been in contact with the Mexicans for centuries, and all but the wildest of them spoke some Spanish. He asked Peshlikai: *"¿Habla español?"*

"Si," Peshlikai said.

"Who is she?" Rim asked.

"Thleen Chikeh," the man answered. "Horse Girl."

"What does she want?"

"She is a strange one. Perhaps she is seeking the wind, or perhaps she is seeking the truth. Both are equally difficult to find."

"You are her brother?"

"I am her betrothed."

As he said this, something came to the surface of his bead-blank eyes, dreaming there like smoke from a campfire. Neither of them spoke for a moment, and then Peshlikai said: "So you are the man who believes John Romaine is a traitor."

It surprised Rim. It was so completely

unexpected. "Where did you hear that?" he asked.

"We hear many things, *Belinkana*."

Belinkana was their word for American. He said it with a sly nasal intonation. Somehow it angered Rim.

"Tell me the truth," he said. "Were you following me that night in Tucson?"

"As I said, *Belinkana*, the truth is difficult to find."

There was no change of expression on his wooden face. Yet Rim had the distinct impression that the youth was smiling at him. Yaki Peters passed them a few feet away, saw the Indian, and called: "Fannin, tell that redskin to git back there with his people."

Peshlikai glanced over his shoulder at the wagon boss, guessed what he had said, and turned to make his way back to the circle of Indians. Horse Girl was visible there, her soft, young body silhouetted by the light of the fire. Rim saw Yaki stop, looking at her. The man's eyes began to shine. He moistened his lips with the tip of his tongue. Then he shambled off toward his wagon.

Lonesome was approaching, and had seen Yaki looking at the young woman. The old man stopped near Rim, rubbing his inflamed eyes. "That Yaki," he said. "I bet we have trouble yet."

Rim did not answer. There was a pattern beginning to take shape, pushing against him like a subtle pressure. And Romaine hadn't wanted him to come.

Before rolling in that night he took out his Navy Colt, checked the loads, and put it by his head. He went to sleep with his hand on it.

Chapter Eight

Up past Rillito, cloud banners swung like ragged pennants from the black-timbered crests of the Santa Catalinas. The promise of more rain rode the fitful gusts of blowing wind. Little dust devils pirouetted over the road and collapsed into crumbling wheel ruts from former wagon trains. The Murphys wound in a creaking, groaning snake of wagon and mule, half a mile long, writhing through a million spines of ocotillo, passing through acres of olive-green greasewood. There was not much to do up there on the box seat of the last wagon except accustom a stiff body to the constant pitch and jerk of the rumbling Murphy and eat the dust of twenty-nine other outfits ahead.

It was the afternoon of the third day when Lonesome's wheel began to scrape. Rim heard it as a thin, screeching sound above the incessant hubbub of the train, and sent his swamper to tell Lonesome. The old man halted his wagon and came back to investigate. Rim was already inspecting the over-heated hub.

"Looks like a hot box."

Lonesome scratched his head disgustedly. "Old man gits a purty gal on his rig, he fergits ever'thing else. How about the tar bucket?"

A bucket of resin, tar, and tallow swung from the tail gate. Rim got it down and they doped the wheel. Lonesome went forward and gave a jerk on his line, starting the team again. They had gone only a few feet when the rear wheel jammed. Cursing, Lonesome halted his team, and once more Rim left his seat to join the man. By now the other wagons had pulled ahead. Calico Mills was outriding for the train and must have seen them halt. He came back, trotting his big patchwork mule. The wound he'd received in the Catalinas was still bandaged and he carried himself gingerly in the saddle. He halted his mule, leaning far back in the cantle of his Mexican cactus-tree saddle, legs thrust forward and outward as if braced against the stirrups. When Lonesome told him what the trouble was, he pawed irritably with the back of a hairy

148

hand at the sweat trickling down his neck from beneath his red beard.

"If you have to take the wheel off," he said, "the others can't wait for you. Them's Yaki's orders."

"But you can't just drop us here alone," said Street. "There's Navajos behind every bush."

"We'll send back a couple of troopers," Calico said. "Watch for the grades ahead. Apache Curve will take every brake on your outfit."

As Calico wheeled and rode off, Rim walked to the head of Lonesome's rig. He told Sherry what had happened. "Maybe we'd better cut out a saddler and let you join the train," he said.

She looked across the sun-baked flats toward the receding train and drew her lips together. Already two dragoons were in sight, riding back toward them. "It looks like we'll be safe," she said. "I think I'd rather stay here."

"It shouldn't take us more'n half an hour."

But it took them longer than Rim had estimated. It was sweating, backbreaking work, the mules braying irritably in the wind, the dust filling their mouths. The jack broke down twice and the linch pin jammed and Street kicked over the tar bucket when they finally got to the axle. The wagon train was out of sight by the time they were ready to go again.

Straightening his aching back, mopping the sweat from his face, Rim looked around him. For the first time the vast loneliness of the land bore in against him. He could see Sherry looking at the horizon. There was a shadow of fear on her pale face, a shrinking look to her body, huddled there beneath the pucker. He sensed what was happening inside her and he knew a compassionate impulse to reassure her. He walked up to the front and she looked down at him quickly, almost furtively. He smiled and pointed at the mesquite forest stretching its hoary growth across the flats.

"You ever run out of food, these mesquite beans would keep you alive for a long time." He indicated a barrel cactus growing beside the road, squat, dark green, leaning inevitably toward the southwest. "Get thirsty," he said, "just cut off the top and squeeze."

"Rim," she said, "I know. Maybe the land will give to some people." She turned away, lips tight, and shook her head. "I can't help it."

He took a resigned breath, turning away. "We'll be up with the train in an hour," he said.

They crossed the river and climbed toward a line of foothills that ran out from the Catalinas. It was higher than it looked and soon the westward desert was spread out below them, carpeted jade green with greasewood. Then they reached a ridge and saw the switchbacks dropping off into a dusky valley. Lonesome halted his rig, and his swamper, a taciturn Papago named Nacho, dropped off and trotted around to set the back action. Rim saw Lonesome helping Sherry down and went up to the head of the rig.

"Sherry kin ride with you," Lonesome said. "If I make it without any trouble, you know she'll be safe."

With the back action lashed, Nacho trotted back and swung aboard. Rim waved his arm at Lonesome and the old man called to his mules: "Gee-up!"

Eight spans of mules leaned into their collars. Four tons of freight shifted and groaned inside the high box with the first forward tilt of the wagon. Rim and

Sherry watched as the high-topped wagon lurched into the grade, rub irons squealing as Lonesome hit the brakes.

The lumbering outfit disappeared around a curve, showed up on a lower switchback. Growing smaller and smaller, the wagon continued down the hairpin curves, finally straightening out on the flats. Rim helped Sherry aboard his seat, climbed up beside her.

"Giddap!"

Leather squawked as the lop-eared mules eased into their collars. Tilting and lurching, the rig began to move. As they rolled onto the grade, Rim put his boot against the brake arm. Rub irons began their shrill protest. The whole wagon was filled with the grumble of shifting freight, the creak of wheels, the shriek of braking. Then the arm jerked against his boot and he lost pressure. Automatically he glanced backward. There was nothing to see. But they were picking up speed.

"You sure you set that brake?" he asked Street.

The tow-headed youth was bending off the seat, trying to see the trailer. "I checked ever'thing."

"I can't feel any back action. Climb back and look."

Sherry sent a troubled glance at Rim as Street clambered back through the pucker, climbing over the crates of guns. They were rolling faster now and Rim leaned against the brake, kicking it hard, trying to feel it out with his foot.

"Whoa, you navvies, whoa!"

Street's shout came from the rear of the wagon. "The brake's gone! Something's happened to the beam!"

Rim kicked savagely at the arm again. The brake beam shuddered as an iron seemed to catch. There was a crazy shriek, then the arm snapped away from him completely. He knew a rub iron had broken free.

"Get off, Sherry," he shouted. "I'll try to stop it with the mules." He yanked the jerk line, trying to turn them into the cut bank. "Haw, you canaries, haw, haw!"

The nigh leader tried to turn in on his companion. But the other mule wouldn't run head on into the cliff. He bit savagely at the nigh leader, jumping his tug chain in wild defiance as Rim pulled on the jerk line again. The whole team was sent into a panic and they heaved into their collars, trying to wheel away from the cliff, ignoring Rim's frantic signals. The wagon was rumbling and bouncing down the grade now and the wheelers broke into a run as it crashed against their rumps. This forced the swingers to run and the panic spread down the line to the leaders. Fighting them, bawling at them, Rim realized Sherry was still on the seat. He had a dim glimpse of his swamper jumping off the trailer. Street hit on his feet, tried to run, tripped, fell flat, rolled hard into the ditch by the cliff. Rim shouted at Sherry. "Jump, while you've still got time!"

She would not react. She clung to the side with white-knuckled fists, staring fixedly at the ground racing by beneath them, frozen with fear. Rim leaned over, trying to shove her off, but she fought him. Fear gave her a savage strength and their struggles almost pitched him away from her and down into the wheelers. He caught the jerking brake arm to keep from falling, pulled himself back onto the seat.

"Sherry," he shouted, "don't be a fool. Jump!"

She lay over the seat, still gripping the

side in fear. Staring at the ground, she shook her head. "I can't. I can't."

He saw now how fast they were going. It was too late, anyway. They were racing down the incline. If she jumped now, every bone in her body would be broken. The leaping, jolting wagon almost pitched him off. The only thing left was the mules. He righted himself, uncoiling his whip, cracking it over their rumps.

"Whoa, there! Haw, Pima! Haw, Yuma! Whoa!"

But they would not slow down now. They were running in panic, with the thunderous roar of the wagon on their tails driving them ever faster. He saw a curve ahead and knew there was only one way to drive them now. If he kept trying to stop them and turn them into the side, they would be so confused on the curves they'd take him right off the edge. He jerked straight back on the line and saw it pull up the leaders somewhat. Then, braying and bawling, they hit the turn. He gave a pair of monumental jerks on the line and bawled at the leaders.

"Gee, there, Pima, gee, gee!"

They wheeled into the turn with the

wagon following. Skidding, leaping, jolting, it wheeled around the curve and into another straightaway. The slope had become a cliff on his left, yawning a hundred feet into a sandy, boulder-strewn wash below. The bank to his right rose in tiered red sandstone to a dusky sky. "Haw, there, Yuma, haw!" A left turn, sharper this time, the rumbling shuddering wagon tilting over till his breath formed a gagging block in his throat. He felt the sudden jerk of the trailer and thought it was going to pull them off.

"Giddap!" he screamed. "Giddap!" The gunshot crack of his whip lashed them into a burst of speed that righted the trailer in the last instant.

They straightened out on another grade. But he heard Sherry gasp beside him. He saw what she was staring at ahead. The next curve was a hairpin, so sharp a wagon would almost have to be halted to make it. He knew a reflection of the sick fear that must be clutching Sherry.

He saw that it was a double switchback. They'd never make the two turns. But the drop from upper to lower road was not steep, if they took it going straight ahead.

"We've got to jump it," he bawled. "Can you chop the trailer loose?"

Sherry looked at him blankly. Fear was a parchment color in her face. He shook her savagely, shouting in a hoarse voice.

"It's our only chance, Sherry. The trailer will pull us over. For God's sake, get back there and knock out the pin!"

He saw her face contort with the pain of his angry grip. Then her face was no longer blank. It filled with a kind of raging anger at him, or at herself, he would never know which. She tore loose, a heated flush filling her cheeks, and scrambled back through the pucker. She tore the double-bitted axe from its sling on the side and crawled across the crated guns toward the rear.

Rim could no longer see her then. The switchback ahead rushed toward them with a volition of its own. They seemed right on it before Rim felt the trailer go. The wagon leaped beneath him, with its release, and he risked a glance backward. Sherry was sagging against the tail gate. The trailer's tongue dug into the ground twenty feet behind the wagon, and the trailer flipped over and off the edge of the road like a feather in the wind.

Dead ahead, the road made its first hairpin curve, running back a hundred feet below them; then it made another turn, switching back again. If he could get it across the rocky slopes onto that bottom road, they would end up going in the same direction they were heading. It took all the will he had to give that one jerk on the line, deliberately turning the mules off onto the slope.

The Murphy reeled and swayed. The right wheel struck a rock and the bed yawed to one side. Rim lashed at his off-swinger.

"Gee, Oraibi, gee!"

The wheeler lurched to the right. Its mate jumped the tug chain to point the same way. Their combined weight jerked the tongue forcefully to that side, pulling the wagon out of its dangerous tilt.

"Pima!" Rim shouted. "Back over that chain! Haw, Pima, haw!"

He emphasized his yell with a crack of the whip. Still galloping headlong downslope, the nigh-swinger jumped back on its own side of the chain. The wagon was leaping and jerking like a fish out of water now. At every new jump Rim was almost thrown off the seat. They crashed onto the first level of the double switchback, but it was going the other way and he couldn't turn without spilling them. The galloping mules hauled the wagon at breakneck speed across the level road and onto the slope behind. Then the rig began bucking and yawing on the rough ground. He had a frantic, kaleidoscopic view of the slope, the sky, the churning rumps of the mules. If one of them went down, they were through. A swinger stumbled and he lashed the animal furiously. The rumble of hoofs and the braying of animals and the crash of the wagon was deafening.

The wagon tilted crazily onto its side, almost pitching him off. He lashed at the mules, getting a new burst of speed from them that righted the wagon. But he knew they could never make the road this way before they turned over. He saw a gully to the left whose mouth opened out onto the road below. It was a desperate attempt. He burned their hides with the whip.

"Haw, Pima! Haw, Oraibi!"

Frenziedly the crazed animals wheeled left, almost upsetting the wagon as they slid into the gully. Deep sand sucked at the hubs and the mules sank to their fetlocks. Rim felt fervent thanks come to his lips as their breakneck speed lessened. It was not enough to stop them. They burst from the gully mouth onto the road, speed slackened enough so that he could turn them without upsetting. Then they were rolling down the straightaway again, with Rim hanging on in exhaustion to the seat. He was dimly aware of Sherry crawling out beside him.

"Jump now," he gasped. "That sand will save you."

She glanced at the hummocks of sand siding the road. Then she looked ahead. They still had one turn before the bottom. He saw little muscles bunch up along her delicate jaw as she clamped her teeth.

"No," she said. "I'll stay with you."

There was a wild exaltation in her face, the kind of look he'd seen in men at the height of battle. The fear and prudery and repression were gone; she was reacting with her most primitive emotions, reacting with the courage and the strength and the passion he'd glimpsed before, through the veil that had always stood between them.

Rolling toward that last turn, he started kicking at the brake arm again and finally heard the remaining rub iron bank against the wheel, giving him momentary pressure, holding them back in that last instant before the curve.

"Haw, Pima! Haw, Oraibi! Haw there, you cross-bred cousins to a calico jack-ass!"

The iron lost contact with the wheel again as they swung the turn. For a moment the wagon skidded, tilted, and they hung on the edge of eternity. Rim burned the hide off the leaders' rumps and they lunged afresh into their collars, digging a cloud of rocks and dust and dirt from the road with their churning hoofs. The burst of speed righted the wagon, pulling it into the straightaway with a monumental jerk.

Rim began kicking at the brake again. Twice more the iron caught the wheel, slowing them down with wild shrieks. He kept a steady tug on the jerk line and slowly the mules responded, heads bumping rumps as each span slowed down. Exhaustion fogged Rim's brain and he was trembling all over with reaction.

In the dust ahead he saw Lonesome's outfit, pulled off the road. They rumbled past the wagon and trailer, slowing down, finally grinding to a halt. Rim sagged over against the seat, unable to move for a while. He was drenched in sweat and the world was spinning. Finally he dropped off and helped Sherry down. He held her trembling body against him and she began to sob uncontrollably.

"I'm sorry, I'm sorry, I don't mean to act like a little girl, but. . . ."

He wanted to cry himself. He looked up at the grade they had come down, the switchbacks they had leaped, and he knew no one would ever believe the telling of it.

"You were wonderful," he said.

She looked up at him, eyes wide, as if sensing the implications of his words. The shining look left her face. A flush touched her cheeks and for a moment he saw something in her eyes akin to embarrassment. She pulled away, making a typically feminine attempt to pat her hair straight.

"I hardly remember," she said. She moistened her lips. She looked away from him, back up that grade, and he saw fright take the flush from her cheeks, and she looked as rigid and frozen as she had when she'd first been hanging onto the seat.

Lonesome and his swamper came running up, and the old man was slapping Rim on the back and hopping up and down like an excited frog. "Boy, howdy! I never seen anythin' like that! You're a mule skinner f'r sure now, Rim."

He broke off as a party of riders materialized out of the dusk. Calico Mills and Lieutenant Denvers and Yaki Peters and half a dozen troopers. Lonesome was still hopping up and down and he launched into a wild recital of what had happened, complete with gestures.

"He did it like he was ridin' on a cloud. Now say he ain't the son o' Sean Fannin. Be haulin' freight t' the moon next, barefoot mice for a team and a barrel o' rotgut for his rig."

The pair of troopers who had been detailed to guard Rim and Lonesome had stopped to pick up Jonathan

163

Street. Now, with the swamper riding behind one of them, they trotted up. Street slid off the horse, running a hand through his straw-colored hair in a helpless gesture.

"Why'ntcha jump?" he asked Rim. "That was plain sooicide. I thought you was gonna jump. Why'ntcha jump?"

"Because he hasn't got a yaller streak down his back quite as wide as yours," Yaki said disgustedly. "If you ain't got the guts to stick with your wagon, I might as well put you on the cavvy and let the wrangler swamp for Fannin. You'll never make a skinner."

Rim saw Street's face turn red with shame and humiliation. It was the worst thing Yaki could have said to the youth. Street looked upon the skinners as gods, and burned with a hope that someday he could handle a whip himself.

"I'll keep the boy," Rim said. "I would have jumped myself if I could."

Yaki glanced sharply at Rim, gaunt face flushing with anger. But Lieutenant Denvers would let it go no further. Reining his mount between them, he said: "We can't stop to argue. Get your rig under way again, Fannin. Calico found Indian sign an hour ago."

Lonesome's exuberance disappeared. The furry seams deepened in his face, making it look infinitely ancient. He peered around at the land, fast disappearing in the pall of night. He pulled his narrow shoulders together within his buffalo coat and plodded back toward his rig. Rim turned to walk back to the rear of his own wagon, squatting down to peer at the brake beam. One of the rub irons had been torn completely off, and the other was dangling. He could see why he'd been able to get intermittent braking. The crossbar itself was loose on the beam and his constant kicking on the brake arm had swung the bar back and forth so the remaining rub iron hit the wheel once in a while. He heard the rustle of Sherry's skirts behind him.

"What happened?"

He rose, wiping tiredly at the grime on his face. "Looks like the king bolt came out of the bar. Which is very strange."

"How do you mean?"

"Things like that don't happen often."

"Are you saying somebody did it?"

"I don't want to hurt you, Sherry. I

165

know it's too soon to talk about it. But you must have wondered yourself why your uncle was killed."

Her face went pale; her lips compressed with an intense restraint. "It was the Indians," she said in a dry, strained voice. "Major Sparks said Uncle Wylie was scalped."

"Anybody can take a scalp, if he wants to plant the blame on the Indians," he said. He saw horror creep into her face, turning her cheeks the color of putty. But he had to finish it now. "I think your uncle was killed because he'd found out something, Sherry."

He saw that she only half-believed him. Yet even that was a gain. Finally she looked down at the dangling rub iron.

"Have *you* found out something?"

"I'm on the track of something," he said. "Maybe it's the same thing Wylie Landor found."

Chapter Nine

They corralled the wagons in the bottoms of the Santa Cruz. Lieutenant Denvers put his pickets out and Yaki set a double guard on the cavvy. In the line, waiting for grub, Calico displayed the broken arrow he had found near the trail that afternoon. He was certain it was Navajo, though the sign he had found with it was a day or so old. It filled the camp with a subdued tension and Lieutenant Denvers had to stop a fight that broke out between two of the skinners. Rim ate with Briggs and Lonesome and Sherry. The Indians ate by themselves near the wagon in which they rode. Rim could hear the purring, turkey-gobble of the three older squaws, and once, when he glanced toward them, he found Horse Girl watching him steadily. Sherry saw it, too.

"You have an admirer," she said.

He grinned at her. "Jealous?"

Her lips drooped and she met his gaze

for a moment; then she looked into the fire and did not bother to answer. He knew the thought of Wylie Landor kept her from pursuing any attempt at humor, and he did not press it. After dinner she retired to Lonesome's wagon. Rim got into a game of freeze-out with Briggs and Lonesome and Steve Swan. They were all so broke, they had to cut Lonesome's chewing tobacco into cubes for the stakes. But Horse Girl was still in his mind and he glanced again toward the circle of Indians. She was not there.

It did not bother him at first. It had been the practice of the squaws to wash in the river at every evening halt, and Denvers had let them go without guards, since there was very little danger of the women's escaping without their men. But when the squaws returned, murmuring among themselves, Rim could not see Horse Girl with them. And a few minutes later he saw Yaki walk past the Indian wagon, his whip dangling around his neck and popping softly against his legs. The man glanced closely at the squaws as he passed. Then he moved, in his shambling, loose-jointed way, to the darkest portion of the circled wagons. Here he stopped and looked back. Rim quickly averted his eyes. When he risked another look, Yaki was gone.

He saw Steve Swan watching him across the tops of his cards. The Southerner's grin was lazy. "Whyn't we take a stroll to the rivah, Yank? I need a wash."

Rim rose with him, and the two of them left the game. Rim saw that Swan had his whip coiled in his hand.

"Your Southern gallantry again?"

"I been watchin' our wagon boss too," Swan said. "She's a woman, Injun or not. I could never look Gen'ral Lee in the eye again if'n I jest stood by and watched somethin' like that happen."

They stepped through the wagons and past the closely guarded cavvy of mules. The Santa Cruz lay like yellow glass under a rising moon and the deep, mucky smell of it was a rare treat in this desert country. They were almost to its banks when they heard the rattle of brush and a soft exclamation farther upstream.

"Don't fight me, you little squaw. It's molasses on the table and I'm havin' some of it whether you like it or not."

It was Yaki's voice. Rim and Swan

169

reached the edge of the willows and saw them struggling in a clearing. Horse Girl had apparently been washing her hair. Like a wet and glossy pelt it swung from side to side in her struggle with Yaki. He had both her wrists in his big, scarred hands, and had forced her to her knees in the sand. She jerked from one side to the other and the black cascade of her hair swung across her face, hiding its crimson anger.

In the pale moonlight, Rim stepped into the open, gun in his hand. "Yaki," he said sharply.

Still gripping the woman's wrists, Yaki whirled toward Rim. His gaunt and bony face was flushed with exertion. A silvery film of sweat lay on the sharp ridges of his cheeks, and a great vein, big as a man's thumb, stood out from his forehead. The woman stopped struggling too, in that moment. Her hair swung away from her face once more as she turned to Rim. Her eyes were immense, the pupils distended like a cat's in rage.

"Maybe you'd like some too, blue-belly," Yaki said.

"Let her go," Rim said.

Yaki looked surprised. Then a slight

light kindled in his eyes. "What's one more Indian, more or less?"

"Let her go," Rim said.

Yaki looked at the gun in Rim's hand. Then with a snarling sound, he swung the woman around in front of him. She was still on her knees, arched painfully backward, and she made a shield that Rim might hit if he fired.

"Now," Yaki said, "if you don't git out, I'll break her in half like a stick."

Rim tried to circle, but Yaki swung Horse Girl to keep her between them. She struggled bitterly, but his great hands held her helpless.

Then, like a hissing black snake, the whip uncoiled from Swan's hand and slithered out on the ground. "Keep movin' around him," he told Rim. "He can't keep her between both of us."

Rim circled farther around Yaki. The wagon boss had to swing the woman again to keep her between them. In a moment Swan would be behind him. Yaki's whip was still coiled about his neck, handle and tip dangling against his legs. With a curse he freed one hand, holding the woman's crossed wrists in the other, and grabbed the handle of his blacksnake. Rim fought his impulse to rush the man. Even with his single hand, Yaki could snap the woman's wrists like tinder.

But Swan had circled till Yaki's back was exposed to him now. With a wild, rebel yell, Swan swung his whipstock back, laying twenty-four feet of braided bull-hide out behind him in mid-air. It cracked like a gunshot and his forearm whipped forward.

But Yaki was quicker. With a practiced flirt, he had laid the length of his whip out on the ground. Without pulling his whipstock behind him for that back-lash, he brought his forearm up in a savage, whipping motion.

As Swan's lash sank toward Yaki's head, Yaki's lash whipped up from the ground to meet it in mid-air, stopping it and winding round and round.

Yaki's attention had gone from Rim in that moment. Still afraid of hitting the woman, Rim rushed in. Yaki heaved the woman at Rim. She fell helplessly back-ward into Rim and he could not stop himself. Her soft body went into his legs, tangling them, and he pitched forward onto his face.

At the same time, he saw Yaki give a mighty heave on the entangled whips, jerking Swan's whipstock right out of his hand. Rim rolled free of the woman, pulling his gun out from beneath his body to fire. But Yaki was already wheeling on him. The wagon boss lashed his forearm viciously across his body, perpendicular to the ground, bringing thirty feet of cured hide up off the ground. The lash cracked against Rim's wrist like the kick of a boot. He cried out with the pain and saw his gun leap from his nerveless fingers. The lash wound around and around his wrist, biting into the flesh with each new coil, and then the lead-weighted bull-horn popper cracked his head a stunning blow.

Sight and sound faded for a moment and he was lost in a vacuum of buzzing pain. He vaguely felt the lash pull free. From somewhere at a great distance he heard the rebel yell again, and knew Swan must have retrieved his whip. Then Yaki's voice filtered through Rim's clouded daze.

"All right, you one-gallus Secesh, let's fry some mule meat!"

Rim rolled over. His face was smeared with blood and his wrist felt broken. Pain and numbness robbed him of will.

He couldn't seem to make his muscles work. When he opened his eyes, he had a vague, watery impression of the two men facing each other, whips in hands.

Yaki held his whipstock up, wrapping those two stiff fingers about it with the others. Then he jerked his arm back, as if to send the lash over his shoulder. It took rare skill to get any effective whip from a snake without first carrying it to the rear for that backlash. But Steve jerked his handle in an oblique upward motion to the right, lifting the whole length of his whip off the ground. Then he brought the braided stock across his body, starting a series of vicious flirts down the length of the whip that would end with the destructive lash of the popper right in Yaki's face.

If Yaki had followed through with his backward, over-the-shoulder motion, he would have been left completely un-protected when Swan's popper struck. But the movement had only been a feint to lure Swan in.

With a vicious reversal, Yaki brought the whipstock back forward, then swept it across the front of his own body. The snapping flirts it sent down his whip brought the whole lash writhing into mid-air to catch Steve's oncoming lash. Steve tried to entangle them, as Yaki had done before.

But Yaki was already jerking free. As Swan's lash dropped to the ground, Yaki pulled his stock back. This time his over-the-shoulder pull was genuine. It gave him all the lash possible in that thirty feet of vicious hide.

Swan tried to meet it, tried to flirt his whip up off the ground to block it. But he was too late. His whip was still a foot beneath Yaki's lash as it came snarling back. In a last wild effort, Swan tried to dodge aside. But the bull-horn popper on Yaki's whip cracked like an exploding shell against Swan's face. Swan's scream obliterated the first words of Yaki's own triumphant shouting.

"That's it, try to paddle your john boat through this. I got you where it counts, let's fry some more side meat, down on your knees, Reb, make some meal for cracklin's!"

Yaki's whip lashed forward again, winding its length about Swan's leg. It tripped Swan and he went to his knees. From there he tried to lash out with his own whip. Yaki tugged back, spilling Swan. The rebel rolled out of the whip and kept rolling. Yaki pulled his whip-stock back over his shoulder, stepping after the man. Sobbing with the effort, Rim got to his hands and knees. He looked for his gun but couldn't find it. Dripping blood from his face, he tried to rise. Dizziness swept him and he fell back onto his hands.

"Put on the skillet, Ma, here comes the 'possum," bawled Yaki. Swan had gained his knees. Yaki's whip cracked him a blow, spilling him flat. Again Swan tried to roll away. Yaki followed. The lash ripped the shirt from Swan's back. It lifted him up and thumped him against the ground with the sound of a beaten drum.

Rim saw Horse Girl run in against Yaki. The man caught her a vicious blow on the side of the head that knocked her away. Then he turned back to the rebel.

Swan was on his knees, mewing and crying like a wounded animal. His bare torso was crisscrossed with lash wounds, smeared and dripping with blood. He was blind and dazed with pain and he scrambled around on the ground like a maddened thing, pawing for his whip and sobbing inarticulate curses.

Yaki's lash sang out again.

"Gee-up thar, General Lee," howled Yaki. "Don't lie down in that bog. Gee-up thar!"

He was shouting in that same, wild exhortation Rim had heard when he'd talked the mules out of the bog. His face had lost all humanity; it was shining with a sadistic ecstasy, and he grunted like a pig every time that lash struck out. It cracked on Swan's face again, turning it to an unrecognizable mass of torn flesh and broken bone. It knocked Swan on his back. In a wild spasm of agony, Swan tried to roll away again. But Yaki wouldn't let him go. Again and again that vindictive lash found his jerking body, ripping it to ribbons.

The ghastly sight seemed to eat through the last of Rim's daze. He stumbled to his feet, groaning with the effort. He heard himself shouting.

"Stop it, Yaki! For God's sake, stop it! You're killing him. Fight a man with two arms, damn you! Leave him go now!"

He stumbled into Yaki, trying to tear the whip free. The wagon boss wheeled on him. His face was loose and shining and filled with a bestial wildness. With a bellow he jerked the whipstock free and cracked Rim across the side of the face with it.

Jolted, Rim tried to hang on, to return the blow. Yaki cracked him again with the heavy stock, knocking him away.

"Damnyankee wants t' see how a mule feels too," brayed Yaki.

Before Rim could recover, that lash came out of somewhere and hit him in the face. The sky exploded. The world rocked on its axis. The earth tilted from under his feet and he slid off.

"That's hit, blister mah tongue if it ain't. Go on, git hup. Doodlebug, stick up your horn. Gee-haw! Gimme an ear now!"

Rim felt as if the whole side of his head had been taken off. He heard himself bawl. Blindly he fought back onto his feet. What had Lonesome said, back by the bog? Something about getting in under his lash. You let him whip at your face and then dive under his lash. He ran at Yaki, but he couldn't even see the lash. He heard it explode and tried to dive beneath it, but the poppers had cracked right in his face and he reeled aside, pawing at ripped flesh and wet blood and eyes that held no vision.

"What's the matter? You hain't afeard of an old coon. Now I'll fry some side meat off that one-armed reb. Come on, Reb, roll in the dirt. All right, pantywaist, here's a dip o' snuff for you. Git on your feet, gawdamn you, stand up and take it. I thought you was the big bully of the ridge."

Stumbling to his feet, Rim saw Yaki's whip leave Steve's belly, and the bloody stripe across the pale, torn flesh seemed to follow the lash as Yaki whirled back toward Rim, and then Rim saw that the lash was red with blood itself, and then the crimson stripe detonated in his face again. His scream came again. His pain. He was spinning. A blow at his back. The whip? The ground!

"I got a gal at the head of the holler, she won't lead and I won't foller. Don't stop dancing. Never saw a double-shuffle like that. Bra-a-ah! Look at that. Crawlin' on the ground like a yearlin' coon, hah! Come out in the spring, coon, hah! I thought you was a mule. I got a lot of hide to take off yet, hah!"

Rim was rolling over. He was being flopped over and over on the ground by that whip and, every time his belly came up or his back came up, there was that snarling explosion and he knew he could not last much longer. He was spinning. Someone was putting a red blanket over him, and the last thing he knew through its agonized suffocation was that raucous voice.

"That's hit. Roll over, coon. Another strip of backfat, hah! Jes' love the smell of burning mule meat. Bra-a-ah! Chicken in the pot, 'possum in the tree, I'll tag you and you tag me. Tag, hah! Look at him furrow that earth. Haw! Jes' a bull tongue plough with a jumping coulter. *Broo-ah! Watch 'at tug! Keepyerchur! Hay, hah! Boo-ah! Bray-ah! Brooo-o-o-o-o-o-a-a-aaaaaaa . . . !*"

Chapter Ten

The guns were booming in the distance when he regained consciousness. He tried to move and pain ran up his leg. Hadn't they got all that damn grape out yet? A stream of jumbled thoughts coursed through his feverish brain. This must be the thirtieth. Why hadn't they pinned Jackson down at Thoroughfare Gap? Now Jackson was on their front and Porter's corps had broken under Lee's Artillery and Hood's Texans had wiped out the Fifth New York. The guns boomed again. Lee must be coming. The realization made him start thrashing in the wagon, because it was dusk and they were racing for the turnpike before Longstreet cut them off and the wagon would overturn and pitch him into that field of dead bodies. . . .

"Rim, Rim, stop it. Quiet down."

The voice in his ear, soft and soothing, and the cool hands on his face brought him back to reality. The names in his mind were no longer Jackson and Hood and Lee. They were Yaki and Steve Swan and Lonesome. He stared up at the Osnaburg sheeting trembling above him on its rusty iron hoops. The booming of the guns resolved itself into the distant crack of mule whips. It was Sherry touching his face. He lay on a heap of buffalo robes and bayeta blankets on top of the crates and she sat beside him, rocking with the wagon, her face pale with concern.

He was conscious of more pain, throbbing, burning. He saw bandages on his hands, felt them on his face. He tried to grin only to find it hurt too much.

"I lost track a while back," he said. "How about filling in?"

She moistened her lips. He could see her recoiling at the memory of violence. She forced herself to speak. "That Indian girl came running into camp. Denvers went down to the river. It took his whole troop to stop Yaki. I think he would have killed you. He was crazy."

"How's Swan?" Rim asked.

She touched his arm. "Just lie easy. Lonesome said it would take a long time to heal. He boiled some oak bark and thickened it with pounded charcoal and

Indian meal. Then he made a poultice from it and tied it on with cowhide."

He frowned at her. "I said how's Swan?"

She hesitated; she bit her lip and looked away. It hurt like fire to move, but he reached up and grabbed her arm, jerking at her. "Tell me, Sherry," he said sharply.

She closed her eyes and her body went stiff in his grip. In a strained voice she said, "He's . . . he's dead, Rim."

For a moment he didn't react. Then a searing rage sickened him and he rolled over. She grabbed him, pulling him back.

"Don't be a fool, Rim. You're too sick and too weak!"

He lay back, exhausted by the effort, dizzy with the pain. He knew she was right. Yet it seemed impossible to lie there, doing nothing, letting it go.

"Is Yaki in irons?" he asked.

She hesitated again. He opened his eyes to look at her, and she answered in a strained voice. "Denvers held a hearing. The Indian girl wouldn't talk. Yaki said he found you and Swan molesting her."

He felt angry surprise. He looked into

her eyes. "Do you believe that?"

She folded her hands in her lap and looked at them. "Of course not."

He saw the doubt in her and tried to sit up again. "Get Denvers."

She caught him, pushed him back. "Rim, you've got to be careful. Every skinner in this train is Yaki's man. Denvers is on the fence. It's Yaki's word against yours. You know what that means."

He subsided again, looking miserably at the rusty iron hoops above him. He knew she was right. On the trail, the wagon boss held a position similar to that of a ship's captain on the open sea. He was next to God. His word was law. His authority was absolute. Even though Lieutenant Denvers held technical precedence over Yaki in certain spheres, the rigid customs and traditions of the trail would give Yaki the upper hand. The teamsters would stand behind him to a man and the young Lieutenant Denvers would be taking a dangerous responsibility upon himself to question Yaki. Even the Indian woman's testimony would have dubious value. Rim knew the prejudice against the Indians, particularly the Navajos.

The Army hadn't believed him in Tucson. Why should it out here?

And Steve Swan was dead.

The anger and the outrage made him sick again. He had liked the reckless, romantic young rebel. Rim had seen death many times. Yet this one seemed so completely, so pathetically unnecessary. And now he was remembering his father. Sean Fannin's shirt had been ripped from his body and his torso had been covered with bloody stripes. At the time it had been thought that Sherod Hunter's men had tried to find the whereabouts of his wagons that way. Now, with a deadly certainty, Rim knew it had not been Sherod Hunter's men. The sickness of rage was gone now, and there was a chill in him, like a core of ice in his bowels. He felt Sherry's hand on him, still restraining.

"It's all right now," he said. "I can wait."

The days followed one another in a dusty cycle, filled with the rumbling of the wagon wheels and the muted rattle and flap of the Osnaburg sheeting in the wind and the soothing hands of Sherry. It seemed that in those days they were closer than they had ever been before; there was no clash, no tension, no quarreling. It gave him hope till he analyzed it. Then he realized how safely she could come to him, with no fear of passion rising between them, no fear of descending to the carnal, the animal, of which she was so afraid.

Denvers talked with him a couple of times. Rim gave him his version, with little hope that it would change things. He knew Denvers was in a bad spot. If the lieutenant put Yaki in irons and it was subsequently found that Yaki was innocent, it could well mean Denvers's stripes. And with Rim out of it and Swan dead, they could not pull another teamster off the train, particularly the wagon boss himself. Denvers said the best he could do was put both Yaki and Rim in technical custody until they reached Fort Defiance, where a trial would be held.

They crossed the Salt, where iron-woods covered the slopes with their mauve bouquets and wild tobacco filled the bottoms with their somber foliage. Up past the river, the highlands of the Mogollon Rim appeared on their left, huddled in a vast, purple shroud of haze.

Rim's swamper had been driving his

wagon, giving the whole train trouble with his thick-witted ineptitude. Twice they'd had to halt for hours because Street had forgotten to dope his wheels and had developed hot boxes. Yaki was for going on, but they were too deep in Navajo country for Denvers to leave a single wagon behind. In this the lieutenant asserted himself and Yaki had to yield.

But finally Rim was able to sit up again and handle his mules from the wagon. That night he saw Yaki for the first time since the fight. With Street jacking the wagon up to dope the wheels, Rim unhitched the mules and led them to water. A dozen other teams were there, spread out along the banks of the Verde, most of the animals standing knee deep in the shallows. The air was filled with their sucking and dripping, the rattle of harness, the tired cursing of skinners. As Rim approached, a man wheeled his dripping spans back toward the holding ground. Instead of passing Rim, however, he stopped. In the darkness his figure was a towering shadow, sway-backed and spread-legged. He held the jerk line and the bit of his off-leader in one hand.

With the other he reached up to grasp one tail of the whip that dangled around his neck. His voice was a lazy, cynical drawl.

"Looks like the ground hog's finally out'n his hole."

Rim did not answer for a moment. He was thinking of the laughing, one-armed rebel, and of the genial, generous Sean Fannin. It seemed absurd that he could stand here so mildly, without expressing his outrage in some explosive violence. It seemed strange that the anger was not a roaring inside him now. Perhaps because it was not really anger any more. It was hate, deep and abiding. A man could hang onto that longer than anger. It would be with him all the time, letting him wait till he was sure of things he only suspected now, allowing him patience for the time and place that he knew would inevitably come. He saw that Yaki was puzzled by his silence, and it gave him the sense of a weapon.

"I guess you talked with Denvers," Yaki said.

"I did."

"Then I guess you know how things stand."

188

"I know." Rim paused. "Do you?"

Yaki didn't answer for a moment. He gave a jerk on the line to quiet the fretting mules. Then he inclined his gaunt frame toward Rim.

"Don't fetch up to me any more, Fannin. It can happen ag'in, any time, any place, and not a whit more fuss raised over it. That's how things stand."

He waited a moment, as if expecting an answer. When Rim did not speak, he jerked on the bit and led his team back to the holding ground.

After watering his mules, Rim left them with the cavvy under guard and went back to the corralled wagons. He found Lonesome by the fire, pants leg up to his knee, pouring hot tallow on his stringy calf.

"Damn jumping cactus," he said. "The fuzzy kind. Why does it allus pick me?"

Rim hunkered down beside him while the tallow cooled. "Dad told me you were pretty sharp with a whip in your younger days."

"That was afore I got the ague." Lonesome snickered. "I could take a red petal off an Indian paintbrush at twenty feet."

"Hiding mules is one thing," Rim said.

189

"Whipping like that is another. How about it?"

Lonesome rubbed his eyes, peering at Rim. "You?"

"Sooner or later, I'll come to it, Lonesome."

The old man shook his head. "No. Listen. Steve Swan was as good with a whip as you'll ever see. What kind of a fight did he give Yaki?"

"Not much."

"That's what I mean. There never was a better man than Yaki Peters. There never will be."

The tallow had congealed now, like a lump of white mucilage on Lonesome's leg. Rim took hold of it. Lonesome's squint dug a million seams into his face. Rim pulled.

"Dammit!" Lonesome said.

Holding the lump of cold tallow, Rim looked at the leg. "Get all the stickers out?"

Lonesome rubbed a hand tenderly across his red calf, still squinting in pain. "I reckon."

Rim threw the tallow into the fire. The flames blazed, spitting like angry cats. Lonesome rolled his pants leg down.

"If you don't show me," Rim said, "I'll learn somewhere else."

Lonesome stared at him. "You're bound an' determined, ain't you?"

Rim nodded soberly. "Did you help bury Steve?"

"No," Lonesome said. "Denvers had some o' the skinners do that, while he was holdin' the hearing."

"There's another heap of rocks back on the Santa Cruz," Rim said.

Lonesome frowned. "Your dad?"

"You know how they found him."

"But Yaki. . . ."

"Was working for Romaine at the time."

Lonesome settled back. "And you still think Romaine made a deal with the rebels."

Rim was silent. From the line before the cook wagon came the constant rattle of tin plates, the rough joking of teamsters. Lonesome wiped his watering eyes.

"All right," he said. "After supper we'll go down in the bottoms."

Chapter Eleven

The banks of the Verde were choked with Spanish dagger and mesquite. They broke brush till they found an open patch. Then Lonesome uncoiled his whip and began Rim's initiation into the more esoteric techniques of the whip.

"First off, the ordinary way. You lay your lash out front, don't you? Then you drag the stock back over the shoulder and lay the whip out behind in the air. Then you bring it back front. That's all right for hiding mules. But it leaves you open in a fight."

"It's what got Steve," Rim said. "He thought Yaki was going back over the shoulder and it sucked him in."

"And Yaki did this," Lonesome said. He sent a flirt down the length of the whip that lifted it off the ground. Before it could drop again he brought the whipstock across in front of him, head high. The whip cracked like a gunshot. Before it could drop, Lonesome brought the stock back in the other direction. For a full minute he kept it in mid-air, lashing it back and forth. Then he let it drop and rubbed his elbow.

"Damn ague. Used to keep it up for ten minutes, never touch the ground. It'll take a stronger arm than you got t' go even a minute. You'll have to practice an hour or so every day before you git the stren'th to put in the kind of session you want. We'll work on the other things, too."

In half an hour Lonesome wanted to quit. Rim let the old man go back to camp while he stayed in the bottoms, not wanting to stop yet. But when he started practicing again, his muscles were like water. The action had re-opened some of the wounds and he felt weak and giddy. He realized he had pushed himself too hard, the first day up. Defeatedly, he started back to camp. Before he reached the brush, however, he stopped.

In the darkness she had not been visible. Now, under the light of a rising moon, he saw her figure silhouetted on a barren tongue of land. The black hair, braided into squash blossoms at the sides of her head, the velvet tunic, outlining the poignant girlishness of her body. Horse Girl.

As in that first time he had seen her, he was impressed by her intense affinity with the elemental sources of life. She seemed to be listening to the wind as it ruffled her voluminous skirts against her copper calves. She seemed planted against the earth, partaking of its secrets.

He broke his way through the mesquite toward her and she did not move. He wondered how long she had been there, watching him. He was on lower ground and had to look up to her, as he stopped a few feet away. She seemed to be quivering, like some wild thing poised for flight. He had failed with Navajo before. He tried Spanish now.

"*¿Por que me sigue?*" he asked. "Why do you follow me?"

Silence. The moonlight, shining against her eyes, turned them to luminous disks in the shadowy oval of her face.

"*¿Que se ofreece?*" he said, almost angrily.

It drew nothing from her. The wind sighed through her skirts and she did not move. The strange, brooding expression of her face, looking down from above, seemed to hold something for him, seemed to touch some sequestered emotion in him that he could not identify. Was this all the communication they could have?

Before he could speak again, the barbaric tinkle and clash of silver bracelets was borne to him on the wind. Rim dropped a hand to his gun as the Indian appeared, moving like a cat through the brush. It was the same dense mesquite Rim had moved through, yet the man did not seem forced to break any of it, or even to brush against it. The only sound he made was that jangle of jewelry.

"Buenas noches," Rim said.

"Buenos noches."

"You should watch your woman," Rim said in Spanish.

Peshlikai answered in the same tongue. "Can one keep the wind in his hand?"

"Why will she not speak?" Rim asked.

"The earth does not speak, yet she has all wisdom."

"You deal in riddles."

"Most men fear the truth."

"I wish to know it," Rim said. "Why did she not talk at the questioning?

195

Why did she not tell that it was Yaki Peters who attacked her, and we who tried to save her?"

"Tried to save her? Or tried to get her for yourselves?"

Rim looked toward the woman, standing silently, a brooding shadow above them. "Is that what she thinks?" he asked.

"Her father died because he believed a white man."

Rim grew angry. "But Swan is dead back there, too."

"Men have died for lust as well as for honor."

Rim glanced back at the woman, trying to find the truth in her face. It was as enigmatic as ever. The motion of Peshlikai's head made his earrings jangle as he looked at Horse Girl. She glanced at the Indian. Then she looked back at Rim. For a moment her lips grew full and pouting and soft. Then she turned and moved like a dark specter toward the camp. Without speaking, Peshlikai followed her. The garish jangle of his jewelry faded and died in the night.

The names. Mogollon Rim. Moqui

Springs. Clear Creek. Canyon Diablo. The Sinks. And to Rim, each name was a commemoration. At the Mogollon Rim he had begun his lessons. At Canyon Diablo he had gained enough strength to keep the heavy whip in mid-air five minutes at a time. At The Sinks he plucked the bud off an Indian Paintbrush at twenty feet.

"That's good, but you got to pull back sooner." Lonesome's voice was in his ears, raucous, querulous, alternately ridiculing and praising. "Only a damn prod-pole greaser would wait that long. You got to gauge when the popper's goin' to hit. Begin your backward pull a mite before. Otherwise your lash drops comin' back. If that was a man, he'd come in overhead. And remember about Yaki. You got to git his legs, son. It's the only way."

There was a radical change to the country above the Little Colorado. The timbered mountains lay behind now, and tableland stretched northward in gigantic grandeur. Titan had scattered his playing blocks over an Olympian carpet and left them for the ages. They rose in sheer mesas from a tawny floor, red as blood in proximity, black as ebony on a silhouetted horizon. Warm, unreal tints of saffron and amethyst wavered across the flats to be swallowed abruptly in the crimson midnight of canyons cut through the sandstone intaglio of escarpments that had taken erosion a million years to sculpt. It was a vast, unknown, frightening country.

It was dry country too, and dust hung thick in the air from the time the first wagon started till the last wagon stopped. It blotted out the sky the morning they left the Colorado. It lay like a veil of golden meal all about Rim, through which he could dimly hear the shouts of the drivers, the creaking of the great wheels, the wheezing of the mules. They had to stop every half hour and swab the clogged nostrils of the animals to keep them going. A wind came up in the afternoon, and blew sand against man and beast like a million stinging knives. Bandannas tied over their faces, hats pulled low, Rim and Street plodded beside the miserable, groaning mules, prodding them with whipstocks and tugging at the jerk line to keep them at it. Rim barely saw the figures on his flank, looming up out of the wind-blown grit like tortured shadows.

They were four horsemen, two of them dismounted. Rim signaled Street and left the swamper to plod by the mules while he veered off to join the quartet. Sergeant Briggs was squatting on his heels in the sand while Calico Mills stood beside him, holding his neckerchief over his bearded lips. Briggs looked up at Rim, spitting sand and cursing.

"This Navajo?" he asked. At first Rim thought the man was holding up a big piece of rawhide. Then he saw that it was a knee-length moccasin, probably discarded when the sole wore through.

"It's a war moccasin," Rim said. "Both the Apaches and the Navajos wear them."

"That's what I figured," Briggs said. "I guess I just wished it was Apache. That wouldn't mean trouble. It'd only be a small party this far west." He frowned at the faded, malleable piece of rawhide. "If it's Navajo, that means Hatali Kintiel, don't it?"

"We're in his country."

Briggs looked at Rim, squinting

against the sand. "You know anything about him?"

"Just the stories."

"You think there's really a man like that?"

"I don't know, Briggs."

Briggs scowled a moment, then glanced sourly again at the moccasin. "I'll take it to the Lootenant."

Rim tramped back to his wagon. The mules were snorting and shying again and, when Lonesome's outfit stopped ahead of him, Rim knew the whole train was halting to tend to the animals again. He was wiping the off-leader's inflamed nostrils clear with a dirty rag when the clank of accouterments reached him out of the haze and in another minute Briggs and a squad of troopers trotted past. The Sergeant reined his horse up, spitting grit, and spoke to Rim.

"Denvers put me on rear guard. You're to close up tight. Put your leaders right on Lonesome's trailer and keep 'em there. If you walk, carry your rifle with you."

"If Denvers is that jumpy, he should stop and corral," Rim said. "They could come five feet from us and we'd never know."

Briggs spat again. "I told him the same thing. But Yaki says there's a spring a mile ahead, and a rim that'll give us protection."

Briggs huddled into his coat, wheeled his horse around, and followed his men. Finished with his mules, Rim tramped up to Lonesome's outfit, back into the wind. He climbed to the seat and leaned inside the pucker. Sherry made a miserable picture, sitting atop the crated boxes, bent over to avoid sticking her head through the canvas top, wiping sand from her ears and the corners of her watering eyes.

"How long will it last?" she asked hopelessly.

"No telling. We'll be under a rim in an hour, though. That'll help some. Anything I can do?"

She shook her head, moistening her cracked lips with her tongue. He hesitated, then heard the order relayed down the line of wagons.

"Stri-i-ng out!"

He dropped off the box and plodded back to his own outfit. His leg had begun to ache again with the walking, and he climbed onto the seat beside Street, who sat huddled over with his face buried in the collar of a buffalo coat. Rim shook out his whip, cracked it above the swingers' rumps.

"Giddap!"

The mules hit their collars and the wagon groaned and began to roll. Then, through the whine of the wind and the sound of sand whipped against the Osnaburg sheeting, Rim heard the shot.

Calico came back through the raging sand, fighting a frenzied horse. Over the bedlam, his hoarse shout was barely audible. "Keep 'em going!" He emphasized the order with a wave of his arm. "Keep 'em going! If we slow down to corral now, they'll cut us to pieces."

Rim knew the man was right. As long as they could hold their line together and travel at the run, the Indians could not pin down the whole train. Yaki probably meant to corral with his back to the cliffs ahead, where they would have water. Rim cracked his whip over the running team.

"Hiyah, mules! Giddap, hiyah!"

As Calico wheeled his whinnying horse to run back down the train, a group of shadowy riders emerged from the blinding sheet of wind-blown sand.

Rim had a dim impression of pinto ponies, naked bronze bodies, drawn-short bows. A feathered shaft drove half its length into the seat beneath Rim. Another pair of arrows whipped through the Osnaburg sheeting. Calico stiffened suddenly on his horse, and then pitched off to one side. Rim saw the feathers protruding from his back before he disappeared in the haze of sand.

Street fired his Yager rifle at the on-coming figures and then grabbed wildly at Rim, panic making a foolish mask of his face. "They're comin'!" he bawled. "They're comin', Rim, they're comin'!"

Rim shook him off, dropping his whip to the foot boards to free his hands for his rifle. The Starr bucked in his hand and he saw one of the shouting figures pitch over the rump of his pinto.

But the others were closing in now, giving him no time to reload. He dropped the rifle behind him, yanking his Navy. With the mules stretched out in a run ahead of him and the wagon bouncing and jolting crazily beneath him, he could get no accuracy out of the revolver. He leveled it across his arm at the nearest rider. The gun bucked. Black powder stung his eyes and smeared his face. He saw that he had missed.

The rider had his bowstring drawn to an ear. The string twanged and there was the whip of wind past Rim's ear. There was a sodden thump and Street grunted sickly. But Rim was already firing again, as a second rider wheeled in, drawing his bowstring. Rim shot three times in quick succession, and on his third shot the Indian fell forward on his horse. His arrow went into the ground and he dropped his bow, hanging onto the mane of his horse to keep from sliding off, disappearing into the cloud of sand.

There were others around the wagon, a jumbled mass of figures, making the air hideous with their war cries and their weird shouts. Rim emptied his gun at another one without making a hit and the man let go an arrow that went through the sheeting a foot behind Rim.

At the same time Briggs appeared. His frenzied horse, frothing at the mouth, was running away with the man, and he had quit trying to stop the animal. The Indians wheeled and broke momentarily before his insane charge. The cavalry horse ran right through the middle of them with the trooper emptying his Colt at their horses. It was the smart thing. At that speed he had little chance of hitting the men. Rim saw two of the Indian pintos go down kicking before Briggs disappeared in the wind-blown sand beyond Lonesome's wagon.

For an instant there was a respite around Rim's wagon. The sergeant's wild charge had broken the group of Indians and they wheeled away, disappearing, perhaps to re-form.

Trying to hold his seat on the bounding, jolting wagon, Rim turned to see Street bent double, hugging an arrow through his blood-soaked middle. Then the boy bent aside and picked up Rim's Navy revolver. He took Rim's powder horn in bloody fingers and began to measure powder into the cylinders.

Then another bunch of howling, chanting Navajos came wheeling like so many hawks out of the storm. Rim saw a trio of them race in against Lonesome's wagon. His breath stopped in him as a flight of arrows cut through the Osnaburg sheeting. In a wild and panicky fear for Sherry, he tore the gun from Street's bloody hands and began firing. The youth had only got three loads seated in their chambers; two of these exploded, causing the gun to buck high in Rim's hand, but the third nipple had become so befouled from the earlier firing that the spark didn't get through to the powder.

He saw that neither of his shots had hit, and now more Indians were wheeling in, against both his outfit and Lonesome's. His fear for Sherry filled him with a rage over which he had no control. He stood in the seat, bawling vile curses at the Navajos, and threw his empty revolver at the nearest rider. It was a futile gesture, for the gun fell far short. In that last, inane moment, while Rim still stood on the foot boards, everything seemed to happen at once.

Street lost his hold on the brake arm and slid off the seat, disappearing. One of the arrows fired by the riders ahead found its mark in Lonesome's off-leader. The mule leaped into mid-air, rearing over to smash against his companion, and then fell, kicking and thrashing. The swingers could not stop and ran right over him, fouling their harness and losing their footing too.

The wheelers went headlong into the tangle, and as soon as the wagon hit them it overturned, plowing a great furrow in the sandy soil and sending up such a gout of dust and grit that it was hidden from Rim.

It was a shocking sight and it drew a wild shout out of Rim. His own mules, completely out of control, veered aside at the last moment from the tangled mess, and Rim's whole outfit had raced by before the dust settled to reveal Lonesome's overturned wagon.

One of the Indians on Rim's flank was still following him. Before Rim could react further to the wreck, the rider raced his pony in beside Rim's wagon and swung aboard on Street's side, a knife in his teeth.

Still on his feet, Rim swung to meet him, throwing himself against the man before the Indian could free his knife. Rim was conscious of the stink of sweat and grease and war paint, of an oily, bronze body writhing against him, of the foot boards pitching and jolting beneath him. Then the wagon yawed and bucked and he lost his footing and pitched off with the Indian still locked to him.

They struck with stunning force and the only thing that saved them was the deep sandiness of the soil. They were jarred loose from each other and Rim flopped and slid down the slope of a ravine, tearing through mesquite, ripping half his shirt off on the rocks, finally coming to a halt at the bottom, so stunned he could not move.

At last, sick and dizzy, he turned over and looked up. The Indian was a vague shadow at the top of the ravine, stumbling through the sand, looking for Rim. He had seen Rim's motion when he rolled over, and he jumped and came down on Rim in a tumbling, sliding run, knife in his hand.

Rim forced himself to his hands and knees. But his will would carry his body no farther. Swaying there, knowing he didn't have the strength to meet the man, he pulled his Bowie from his boot and took a long chance.

When the Indian was but ten feet away, with his stumbling feet kicking sand down into his face, Rim threw the knife. It was an overhand, Mexican throw and it buried the blade hilt-deep in the naked brown belly.

The Indian doubled over and came

falling into Rim, knocking him over on his back. But the Indian's body was a slack weight on Rim, and he writhed from beneath it, covered with the man's blood.

Rim crawled away a few feet and lay on his belly, groaning with pain and utter exhaustion. Dimly he saw the Indian roll over onto an elbow, holding one hand against the knife in his belly without making an effort to draw it out. In a moaning voice, he tried to sing.

Blood began to bubble from his mouth and he choked on it and had to stop. He lay on one elbow, breathing shallowly, swallowing the blood and trying again. Rim realized it was his death chant.

This time the blood broke from his mouth in a purple gout and he doubled over, twitched his knees, and died.

Rim turned away. Finally he started to crawl up the slope. It took him an eternity. He had to stop often, dizzy and weak. Finally he reached the top and got to his feet and did not fall.

All he could hear was the dismal howl of the wind. There were no shots, no war chants, no rumbling wagons. His fear for Sherry was like a nauseous pressure in him, and it drove him stumbling through the sandstorm toward the overturned wagon. He did not know how long it took him to find it — half an hour, maybe. He had to circle back to the ravine twice for his bearings.

But finally he found the first rifle case. It had been broken open and rifled of its contents. Farther on another, and another, a whole trail of them leading to the tangled wreckage of the Murphy and its trailer, with the sand already heaping drifts against its smashed box.

Two of the mules had been cut free of the harness by the Indians. The one with the arrow in its vitals and the others, rendered useless by broken legs, had been left to die. The Osnaburg sheeting had been ripped off and more crates were scattered about, emptied of their rifles. Rim found Lonesome beneath the seat, dead. He tore his way through the wreckage and then wandered around in a great circle, half hysterical from his exhaustion and his fear. He called for Sherry, again and again. There was no answer.

He finally stumbled back to Lonesome's body and dropped to his knees by the man. He crouched there, drained of energy, trying to focus his mind on some goal. His empty eyes watched the sand softly drift over Lonesome's body. The old man was almost covered now.

Finally Rim shifted through the drifts till he found Lonesome's boot, pulling his Green River skinning knife out. Then he made himself go to the mules, slitting their throats to put them out of their misery.

He knew how foolish it would be to wander out in the sandstorm. The chances were a hundred to one that he'd lose his way and be finished for good. But the possibility that Sherry had done the same thing, that she was out there somewhere, would not let him remain here. He hunted for Lonesome's Yager rifle in the wreckage, but could not find it; he pawed through the smashed wagon for the canteens, could not locate them.

Then, with nothing but the old man's knife in his boot, he started off in the direction in which he thought lay the rim and the springs. The sand covered the wagon trail completely. He stopped every few feet, listening, calling for Sherry. The lonesome whine of the wind was his only answer.

He came upon the bodies suddenly. If any Indians had died, they had been carried away by their fellows. All that was left were the troopers. It looked as if this was where the lieutenant had put up his big fight. The bulk of his command lay here, sprawled on their bellies or pinned beneath dead horses or lying on their backs and staring up at the sky with sightless eyes and gaping mouths. And they had all been scalped.

Rim had seen more carnage than this at Gaine's Mill, at Shiloh, at Manassas. But somehow the sight of those grisly heads gave a macabre significance to death that no other battlefield had attained for him. He stood there alone in the howling wind, sickened, outraged, watching the sand sift its mordant cerements over their remains.

"You poor bastards," he said.

He didn't want to go on. He didn't want to see any more. But now he had to know. So he walked again, his back turned to the sand that whined against him, biting the exposed flesh of his neck, sifting into his ears, sawing against his cheeks till they felt on fire. He passed more huddled, blue-coated bodies, already half buried in sifting sand. Then there were no more. At last he tried to circle back and regain his bearings. But he could not find his way. He came across no more signs of the battle, no more bodies. He circled until the wind-blown sand began to darken. He knew that night was descending.

He was lost. He forced himself to admit it. He was lost and night was coming. He circled again, through the lowering darkness, till he found a lonely saguaro. It would give him meager protection against the sand, but it would be better than nothing. He huddled down in its lee. The thought of Sherry was still with him, poignant as a knife thrust. But he was helpless now. He could do nothing for her, nothing even for himself. All he could do was wait for daylight. A stupor of exhaustion closed about him, and fear and frustration succumbed at last to sleep.

When he awoke, it was light again. The wind had stopped blowing. The sand was drifted over him, but he could see the sky, like a pale green sea rolling over the world.

Sunrise gave him his bearings again. But he had wandered too far. He marched in ever widening circles from the saguaro, seeking the scene of battle. But he could not find it. The sand had covered everything, even his own tracks of the night before. He was burning with thirst now, weak from hunger. Near noon he thought he saw a river and spent an hour traveling toward it, only to have the water become a bed of sand. A mirage.

He stood there in the hot sun, dizzy and weak, facing the terrible decision he would have to make sooner or later. He could do Sherry no good wandering aimlessly in the desert. He would not last much longer at this rate. The chances were that if Sherry still lived, the Indians had her. The thought filled him anew with anger and outrage; yet he had to face it.

By the best calculations he could make, Fort Defiance was the nearest white settlement, some eighty miles northeast. There would be troops there, to come back with him in his hunt. If he could find water, he could make it. He looked behind him once. His face grew bleak and empty.

"Sherry," he said.

Chapter Twelve

Probably the most dangerous portion of the United States in that year was the country north of the Little Colorado. Here, in this burned and broken land, a whole people had been conditioned by hundreds of years of ceaseless warfare to kill a white man on sight. On every side of this section — from the country of the Taos Indians north of Santa Fe to the land occupied by the descendants of the Aztecs in Mexico City — lay the tribes subdued by the Spanish *conquistadores,* converted by Franciscans, and finally held in subjection by the American Army. But in four centuries these three races of conquerors had failed completely in their efforts to subdue the Navajos north of the Little Colorado. And it was into their domain that Rim moved.

He knew the risk he took. But it was his only chance for survival. He saw more mirages that afternoon but finally he found a field of barrel cactus and cut the tops off with Lonesome's knife, sucking the pulp dry of its moisture. This kept him going till nightfall. He found a *tchindi* hogan and slept there, knowing he would be safe, for no Navajo would approach one of their dwellings in which someone had died. The body was always taken out through the north wall and the wind howled through this hole all night long, like the moaning of the lost souls which were thought to inhabit these hogans of those who walk by night.

Dawn splashed a cardinal hue over the sky. As Rim started his march again, the sun changed, from red dawn to blinding white day. He crossed miles of dun flats dotted with olive greasewood, came up against the wall of a mesa so high he could barely see the top. He found a gash cut through this by some ancient upheaval and groped his way into it, the walls reeling above him till their tops seemed to touch. He came out onto a plain that sloped upward toward a distant rim, covered with a mesquite forest. The beans littering the ground were last year's crop, dried and rancid, but he knew the nourishment they contained, and gathered a hatful to eat on his way.

The sun began to affect him. He felt as though his brain were frying. He caught himself stumbling and veering and then, for the first time, he fell to his knees.

He was hazy about that night. He could find no shelter on the vast plateau and spent most of the dark hours sprawled flat on the bone-chilling ground, sunk in a stupor of exhaustion. The next day he grew delirious. He seemed to spend hours in silly laughter at a jack rabbit hopping across his trail. He sobered himself with the ludicrous dignity of a drunk.

Time lost meaning. Two days now? Three? He didn't know. He slept again. Or maybe he just passed out. When he regained consciousness, it was day again. The sky was again blinding white and the sun burned his brain till he held his arms over his head, stumbling through acres of glaring, yellow sand. Then there were chocolate-colored buttes and a sandy wash and there were four rainbows, each one forming the side of a rectangle. Farther on, colored sticks were thrust in the ground with something like faces painted on their upper ends. And a glittering piece of turquoise.

Navajos? Was that it? And a spring. Was that it? The way they prayed for water, at a spring. Making sand paintings of rainbows. He started digging in the sand, grunting and whimpering in animal eagerness. But there was no water. Finally he stopped, panting, the sweat dripping from him. And he heard the noise.

This time it was no shrieking Parrot shell, no crackling Confederate musketry. It was a noise that belonged to the desert, and to reality. Soft, sliding, insistent. Like someone moving furtively through the sand.

He looked around. He was at one of their springs. It was logical. Their sign was all about him. The sand painting, the turquoise, the colored sticks. It was logical. And all he had was a knife.

He was pitifully exposed, in the bottom of the wash. He looked about frantically. Ahead was a strip of black lava. Beyond that lay a strange, rock-like formation. It was like the trunk of a tree broken into sections. Beyond it lay another, unbroken, the gnarled and serrated surface glittering in the faithful reproduction of tree bark. He rose and stumbled toward them, dropping to his knees behind the first giant trunk. He touched its rough surface. Stone.

He knew what it was now. His father had seen it, on the way to Santa Fe. A petrified forest. Acres of giant trees that had toppled ages ago and had turned to stone before man was known to the earth.

Through the years, bits of the fallen giants had broken off to cover the ground with a layer of glittering, polychromatic chips. His slightest move made a grating sound in this rainbow mosaic. He heard the same sound from somewhere else.

Like something jerked on a string, his head swung around. The noise came again, soft, grating, insistent. In a sudden, delirious panic he rose and ran. Stumbling ankle deep through the creamy chalcedony littering the ground, slipping and falling in shimmering butterfly chips, crawling across the brutal knife edges of yellow agate, he made his way blindly through the prehistoric grove. He fell headlong behind another of the toppled, broken trees. He tried to rise again and couldn't. It was pain to breathe. Hunger and exhaustion left him no strength. He was giddy and sick.

Over the husky roar of his breathing he heard the crunch of feet in the layer of chipped rocks. Sobbing for breath, he pulled Lonesome's skinning knife. Then the crunching in the rocks blended with another sound. Like the tinkling of little bells. A barbaric, jangling sound. It couldn't be! He must be delirious. He raised his head, trying to focus his eyes on movement twenty feet away. It became a man. It became Peshlikai, the silversmith, standing there with a rifle in the crook of his elbow. In Spanish he said: "You will come with us now."

Rim remembered little of the ride. They pushed hard, seeming to travel unceasingly, giving him no time to recover from his exhaustion and shock. The delirium stayed with him, making it a trance-like journey, filled with illusory impressions of a vast, wind-swept land that stretched forever into a blinding sun — yellow sand and red mesas and tortured canyons. There were blank stretches when he must have ridden in a stupor, held in the saddle by the pair of half-naked Indians who rode on either side. There were other, more lucid moments when he saw Peshlikai riding like a shadow on his flank.

When they did stop, he was so spent that he slept like a dead man during the whole halt. Then they were up again, giving him a handful of green, parched corn and a twist of mutton to eat, hoisting him into the saddle.

The thought of escape came often. But he was too weak and too confused to fight, and those two braves were always at his side, silent, hostile, implacable. Then it was night, with ragged cloud banners hiding the moon. In the pitch blackness they entered a canyon. The vague sense of its vast walls was like a chill pressure against him. They crossed a broad and shallow stream, clattered through rocks, waded through sand. Then he was helped off the pony and pushed onto a trail that shelved forever upward. Beneath him, in the blackness, lights winked like the reflection of stars, and he thought of campfires. Once a dog barked, deep in the pit, and the echoes beating against the walls turned it to the baying of a thousand giant hounds.

He stumbled and fell a score of times, a hundred. He was wheezing and dizzy with exertion when the trail finally leveled off. He was forced to stoop by the two guards and almost pitched headlong through a low door. He went to his hands and knees and saw a wall behind him and rolled over into a sitting position, seeking its support.

He was in a cave, with the light of a fire licking up over its stone walls. And beyond the fire, squatting on his haunches with all the relaxed indolence of a sleepy bear, was a man. Over broad, bunched shoulders he wore a *yei* blanket. Beneath it Rim could see he was naked save for a buckskin loincloth and a pair of hip-length Apache war moccasins, folded over so that they extended to knee height. His face was the color of old copper, brutally formed, like something hacked out by an angry sculptor.

The nose was a hawk's beak; the cheekbones had an Oriental tilt, running in sharp ridges against the flesh. The thick carnality of the lips was mocked by the Machiavellian cunning of brilliant eyes. He had a sly, jester's smile.

"Ahalani, Belinkana," he said.

"No habla navajo," Peshlikai said in Spanish. "He does not speak Navajo."

"We will speak in Spanish, then," the other man said. "I am Hatali Kintiel."

It came as a distinct shock. Rim hauled himself a little higher against the wall, staring at the Indian. Hatali Kintiel. A name of hate and fear and mystery. A name mentioned in hushed whispers around every campfire between Chihuahua and Salt Lake City. A name that would rank with Geronimo and Cochise and Mangas Coloradas, when the history of this bloody era was written.

And yet, to Rim's knowledge, no white man had ever seen this Indian who squatted before him over the snapping fire. Kintiel must have sensed what was going through Rim's mind, for a pawky grin spread his carnal lips. Then he spoke to someone beyond.

The guttural Navajo words brought a squaw out of the darkness behind Rim. Like a shadow she moved to a heap of dishes in one corner. The Navajos traded their peerless blankets to the Pueblos for pottery. Into the dishes the squaw ladled greasy mutton from a red-hot stew kettle standing by the fire. From under a mat she fished bread made of yellow maize, and onto this smeared cactus syrup from a jar. She handed the food to Rim. Hatali Kintiel spoke again, in the guttural, swallowed language of his people. The squaw stooped through the door. Peshlikai seemed to hesitate. He looked at Rim with those insolent, bead-black eyes. Then he wheeled and went out.

They were alone.

Rim held the plate, watching the man. Kintiel gestured at the food. Rim began to eat. The greasy mutton made him a little sick at first, but he was ravenous. Kintiel rose. He was no taller than average. His thighs were strong and muscular, but the tremendous barrel of his torso made him look bandy-legged. He even moved like a bear, with an indolent shuffle, rolling his bulky shoulders from side to side. He circled the fire, studying Rim.

"You wonder," he said, "why you have been brought here."

"Is that not natural?"

Kintiel stopped. He smiled. "You are the one who believes John Romaine a traitor," he said.

Rim stopped eating. It was the same thing Peshlikai had said to him that night on the trail, almost the exact words. It was a key turning in a lock, a door beginning to open. Kintiel sat down again, cross-legged, like a crafty Buddha.

"What is your name for the men in the gray suits?"

"The Confederates?"

"The Confederates." Kintiel nodded. "A year ago one of them came to my people. He agreed to supply us with arms and ammunition if we would fight you. He agreed to inform us where wc could attack, without meeting your soldiers, where the most loot was to be had, where we could hurt you most. In particular, he wanted us to stop the operation of your gold mines."

Rim set the plate down, staring at the man. "Did he say why?"

"No. And I do not understand, myself. What would it mean to the blue coats, if the gold no longer came from the ground?"

Rim was beginning to see now. He knew the war had bled the Union dry, that the federal treasury was dangerously depleted. In this last year, the

Arizona gold fields had become of such prime importance to the government that there was a bill before Congress to create a territory separate from New Mexico. It added up. If those gold fields were lost, it would be as important a victory to the Confederacy as a major defeat of the Union armies in the field. Excitement stirred in him. This was one of the answers he had sought so long.

"This Confederate agent who came to you," Rim asked. "Who was he?"

"One named Dee Bartlett."

Rim was silent as more pieces fell into place. He remembered Bartlett's mysterious presence at the Catalina mine during the Navajo raid, remembered Corsica's fear and pleading.

"But he is only a go-between," Kintiel said. "One of a large group that sympathizes with the gray suits. At the head of his group is a leader, unknown to us."

"John Romaine?"

"I do not know."

"But surely Romaine is involved. What about the sand he was carrying to the Pima Indians?"

Kintiel nodded. "Your people had already failed to keep their treaty with the

Pimas. You did not take them the winter beef that was promised."

"Romaine had a hand in that. He contracted to deliver the beef, then claimed it was rustled on the way."

"And because of it, many of the Pimas starved and were sickened. They had great hate in their hearts for your people. There was talk of war in their villages." Kintiel became an orator, using sonorous phrases of surprisingly fluent Spanish, making broad, theatrical gestures. "If that sand had reached the Pima camp instead of flour, it would have been final proof that the white man spoke with a forked tongue. The Pimas would have revolted. They would have joined the Navajos in our war against you."

All of which could fit into the larger picture of the Confederacy's plan, Rim realized. There wouldn't have been a friendly tribe left in the territory. The whites were already hanging on by the skin of their teeth, with Tucson the only major outpost left. It was hard for him to grasp. All the time he thought he'd been trying to uncover Romaine's corruption; the true scope of what he had been digging at was staggering.

"Is that why they killed Wylie Landor?" Rim asked. "Had he stumbled across this?"

"Perhaps he had even found out who their leader was."

Rim stared blankly into the fire. If it was true, it justified all his groping, all his searching, his questioning. It was as if he were no longer lost, wandering, suspecting something, yet not knowing what he suspected. It gave him something to get his teeth into and for a moment it wiped away all the restlessness, the bitterness he had known in Tucson. His foe was no longer a nebulous, veiled thing that mocked him with hidden laughter and half-truths; he had come to grips with it at last.

Then he looked at Kintiel. Slyness had left the man's stony features. In the ruddy firelight his face looked like that of some cruel, brooding god. And new suspicion took the bottom out of Rim's triumph.

"Why should you tell me all this?" he said. "Why should you bring me here at all? Why didn't they kill me like the others?"

The man raised his head. As he looked into the Machiavellian brilliance of those eyes, it was hard for Rim to believe that this man was a savage.

"In time," Kintiel said, "perhaps you will know." He looked at Rim a moment longer, then pulling the *yei* blanket about him, he rose. "You will sleep now. We will talk again."

"Before you go," Rim said. "There was a woman with that wagon train."

"A friend of yours?"

"More than that."

"The war party is not back yet."

"Didn't they bring me in?"

Kintiel shook his head. "Peshlikai was not with them when he found you. After the fight, he and the two others stayed behind to seek you. They discovered your tracks when the sandstorm was over."

"Then the war party should have got here ahead of us."

"They are a bigger group, and did not push night and day as Peshlikai did. We will learn of your woman when they return."

Chapter Thirteen

There was a heap of grimy bayeta blankets in the corner of the cave-like room. After Kintiel left, Rim finished his meal and then made a bed for himself. There were a thousand questions in his mind. He thought his fearful concern for Sherry would not let him sleep, but he was exhausted. The questions faded, but his last conscious thought was of her. . . .

When he awoke, the fire was dead and the room was chilled. Daylight crept beneath the rawhide covering of the door and feebly outlined the heap of pottery in the corner, the circle of blackened fire stones in the center of the floor. There was the smell of mutton and smoke and dank earth in the cave. Rim threw his blankets off and got to his feet. He was stiff and sore and ached all over. Wind and sun had burned his face till it felt like cracklings and was tender to the touch. He pushed aside the hide covering the doorway and stepped outside. He took one step and then recoiled, almost pitching backward into the room. Another foot and he would have plunged over a precipice into a void, seemingly without bottom.

He was standing on a ledge, on the wall of the deepest canyon he had ever seen. With his first introduction to Hatali Kintiel, the night before, he had known that he was in Canyon de Chelly, the infamous Navajo stronghold. But he hadn't realized the position the little room occupied. It was nothing more than a cave hacked out of the rock, reached by a trail that ran like a shelf up the sheer precipice from a thousand feet below.

He moved so that his back was against the cliff and then looked below once more. The void was not without bottom. The canyon floor lay an incredible distance below him. Sand flats made a bone-white gleam down there, and the placid mirror of a river wound between the patchwork quilt of corn and alfalfa fields. On either side of the river were clusters of hogans, looking as tiny as the tip of Rim's little finger, and the jackstraw pattern of corrals.

The canyon itself wound in either direction like a tortured snake, splashed red near its rims by the rising sun, steeped in purple shadows in its depths, so narrow in some places that the walls seemed to touch at the top. This was the fabled Gibraltar of the Navajos. Until 1690 the tribe had been nomads wandering in the desert country east of Chelly, a people of scattered clans, with no core and no strength. Then, fleeing the fires of the Spanish reconquest, they had sought the canyon. Here, literally, was the birthplace of the Navajo nation. Sheltered from their enemies, with a place to herd their stock, they thrived and grew. Within one generation they had filled the canyon and overflowed into the cornland outside. Chelly was considered so impregnable that only once did the Spaniards venture inside. What happened then gave a tributary gorge its name of *Cañon del Muerto* — Canyon of the Dead. And never again was the stronghold assaulted. With this assurance of safety, the Navajos raided and looted all the tribes around them until their name was a word of dread from Santa Fe to Chihuahua.

Rim realized he was looking at something that few white men had seen. It was like being the first man on earth. It was breathtaking, gripping Rim in its terrifying grandeur, filling him with such an awe that he failed to see the tiny figure laboring up the trail from below. Not till the man had stopped, a hundred feet below him, did Rim take notice.

He was old, with a face seamed by time and weather. His gray hair was coarse as the mane of a horse, held back from his forehead by a *banda* of blue wool. He was barefooted, and his only garment was a tattered military greatcoat of faded blue, buttoned to the knees. He sent a fearful look at the door of the cave, then spoke in a shrill squaw's voice.

"Ha at iish binighe yiniya, Belinkana?"

"No habla navajo," Rim said.

"Ai!" The old man nodded wisely, coming a step farther. Here he stopped again, moistening his lips. "Are you a witch too?" he asked in Spanish.

"Do I look like one?"

"You go into the *tchindi betatakin* . . . the witch house. Hatali Kintiel is the only other one who does that. He married a woman within his own clan."

"Does that make him a witch?"

"Of a certainty. And now he lives in this place occupied by *tchindis.* They are devils who haunt the places where people have died. If a man dreams of a bear or *tchindi,* he will sicken and die. This house in the rock shelf was built by people who lived here before the Navajos came. They dreamed of *tchindis.* That's what happened to their whole tribe. There was nothing left of them when we came here. Nobody but a witch or devil-worshiper could live in one of these places and survive."

"I thought you people killed your witches."

"Many would like to do away with Kintiel. They would if he were not so powerful. They have great fear of his witchcraft."

Somehow, this old man, with his seamed face and his shrill loquaciousness, reminded Rim of Lonesome. "Who are you?" he asked.

"Kintiel ordered that I am to be with you while you are here," the old man said. "I am to answer your questions and help you with our language and see that you are not harmed. I am Gontzo." The ancient indicated a swollen knee.

"It means Big Knee. I fell off a horse in a fight with *Ahdilohee*."

"Who's that?"

"It means the Rope Thrower. It is our name for the man you call Kit Carson. This is his coat I wear." The old man stuck out his chest proudly. "I took it from him in battle. I would have had his scalp, too, if I hadn't broken my knee in a fall off my horse. I was a great warrior in those days." His grin faded and he sighed wistfully. "Have you a piece of meat? I am tired of the rodents we dig out of their holes. It is getting so bad only the headmen get mutton now."

"There is some meat in the cave," Rim said.

He saw fear pinch Gontzo's eyes almost shut. The old man stared at the mouth of the cave and Rim could see hunger clashing with superstition. Then Gontzo shook his head sadly.

"I could not eat meat from the *tchindi betatakin*. I would surely die."

Rim sidled down the trail, hugging the wall. "Then I will ask Kintiel to get you some meat from below, if you will tell me about the war party. Have they returned?"

Gontzo nodded. "Early this morning."

Rim was unable to keep the tension from his voice. "Is there a white woman with them?"

Gontzo shook his head. "That I do not know."

"Can we find out?"

"It would be dangerous for you to go down there. As Kintiel's prisoner, you will not find favor among those below."

"I've got to find out."

They were standing at the edge of the shelf, looking down in the chasm of the canyon's floor. The old man pointed toward a tall, spindle-like monument, a narrow and extremely tall mesa, thrusting as a forefinger directly upward into the sky.

"Do you see that tall, narrow mesa?" he asked Rim.

"Yes."

"The People call it Spider Rock. In the ancient days, there was a huge spider who lived on top of that high mesa, and the spider would fling down his web and snatch those who passed his rock. That is what happened to the white woman. The huge spider has her atop Spider Rock. Perhaps, when we celebrate *konc ah-leel'* — the fire dance — you will find her. Perhaps then the spider will release her."

"Is she somewhere down below?" Rim asked, his tone insistent. "I can see the top of Spider Rock from here. She is not there."

"You ask what I do not know. That you cannot see something does not mean that it is not there. Many things cannot be seen. The *tchindis,* the dark walkers of the night, cannot be seen, but they can be heard, and they can be felt."

"Will you go with me, there, down below?"

"I have been ordered to be with you while you are here. I have told you it is dangerous below, among the clans. If you will go below, I shall go with you."

"*Gracias,*" Rim said, his eyes squinting in the white light, feeling both grateful and perplexed.

It took them a long time to reach the bottom. Rather than follow the trail all the way down, Gontzo showed Rim short cuts of hand and footholds that ran vertically down the cliff. It was a vertiginous, precarious descent and Rim reached the bottom damp with sweat and trembling with strain. On a sand flat a hundred yards away was a cluster of hogans. As Rim and Gontzo went through them, the other Indians began to gather. Women pushed aside door blankets of woven yucca stalks and stepped out. Men standing at the jackstraw corrals turned to look, and then moved together. They were all thin and stringy, the copper of their bodies grayed with caked dust. Few of them wore shirts; their leggings were buckskin, and some wore only loincloths. They wore their hair long, tied in two squash-like knots at the back of their heads. With a soft rustle of moccasins in the sand, a muffled tinkle of hand-hammered silver, they gathered.

Gontzo was silent, looking apprehensively from side to side, hurrying through the village. As they left the hogans, Rim saw that one of the Indians was following them. It was a woman, reed slim in her blue velvet tunic and heavy skirt. With surprise, he recognized Horse Girl.

Gontzo chuckled. "She is a shy one. Gone like the wind if you approach her. Always alone. Always off in some canyon gathering wood or sitting on some rim watching *Johano-ai* riding across the heavens with his golden disk."

"Does she never speak?" Rim asked.

"Rarely. But once I did hear her singing *hozhoni* songs. She has a voice like silver bells." He nodded slyly. "There are many young men who would like to have her in their hogan."

"I thought she was betrothed to Peshlikai."

Gontzo looked at Horse Girl. "Sometimes I wonder," he said.

They reached the river. Placid as glass, the water flowed through the fields of corn, winding back and forth across the irregular floor of the canyon. Here Rim stopped, looking back at the woman. She stopped, too. A sun flush lay like rouge on her copper cheeks and her hair drank in the light, so glossy-black it looked wet. She seemed to sway a little, like a young willow in the wind. Finally Rim and Gontzo moved on. Only then did she follow, shyly, starting and stopping, like a young doe picking its way tentatively into a glade.

Gontzo pointed to another cluster of hogans in the ice-blue shadow of the great wall. "Ahead is the village of the Bead Clan. We will find Standing Waters there. He led the war party that attacked your wagons."

A dozen men and women had formed into a loose group before the hogans by the time Gontzo and Rim reached them. One was a man of uncommon size for an Indian, taller than Rim, with a great, beefy chest that gleamed like tarnished brass in the early morning light. Across that chest ran a fresh scar, livid and ugly, and his left arm was tied with a blood-stained bandage.

"That is Standing Waters," Gontzo told Rim.

"Ask him about the white woman," Rim said in Spanish.

Gontzo approached the tall Navajo like a sycophant before his emperor, cringing and smirking. *"Ahalani, Belegana yiyisgini,"* he said.

Standing Waters had a booming, pompous voice. *"Ahalani, Gontzo. Ha'at iisha."*

There was more talk. Gontzo seemed to be approaching the subject circuitously. Finally Rim heard the words *Belinkana ah-dzah'nih* — American woman. He saw a faint flush run into Standing Waters's broad, flat cheeks. He answered angrily, a long, garbled sentence. Gontzo moved backward, looking over his shoulder at Rim.

"He says he knows nothing of the American woman. Shall we go now?"

It was all too abrupt. Rim saw Horse Girl standing at the edge of the group, her great, black eyes fixed on him. When he met her gaze, her eyes fluttered away like frightened birds. For a moment they touched one of the hogans, then darted to Standing Waters.

"I'll bet she could tell us something," Rim said. He started toward her. Before he had gone two steps, he heard someone speak from within the log house at which the woman had looked, a low murmuring voice, bitter and hopeless.

"No, no, I won't."

He stopped. He would have known that voice anywhere. It was Sherry.

Gontzo shouted at him as he ran toward the door, but he didn't hear what the old man said. He tore aside the mat of tightly woven yucca stalks. He had to stoop so low, plunging through, that he went to one knee just inside. The interior was dark, and the rancid stench of mutton and old hides and body odors gagged him. It took his eyes a moment to accustom themselves. He heard the babble of voices outside and the pound of feet toward the door. Then the two figures huddled against the far wall took form for him.

One was Sherry. He had that moment's dim impression of her. She had been stripped naked and her dress was nearby, soiled and rumpled and ripped in a dozen places. Her white skin gleamed in the semi-darkness, but bruises were visible. Her face was scratched and smudged, hollow-cheeked with fatigue. Her long hair hung over her face in a honey-blonde cascade, hiding her eyes, and she was crouched on her knees in a heap of bear robes and blankets, a figure of abject humiliation and defeat. A tubby squaw in a rawhide skirt had apparently been trying to pull her to her feet. She still held Sherry's arm, but she was turned to Rim in owl-eyed surprise.

Rim had that instant in which he saw them. Then he heard the grunt of a man stooping through the door behind him. He was grabbed by the arms and pulled back through the low door and flung on the ground.

They were all about him, a circle of dust-grayed bodies and angry brown faces and the guttural babble of their exotic tongue. Swaying directly above him was Standing Waters, his thick lips twisted, his eyes blazing with anger. Rim had no sane thought left in his head; his whole, wild impulse was to get Sherry out of this. With a husky, animal sound he rolled over and threw himself at the door again. His lunge knocked aside a pair of braves standing before the opening.

He was caught from behind again, while still on his hands and knees, and thrown back once more. This time, as he fell to the ground, they were upon him, kicking and pummeling. His body flopped over with their blows and he grunted sickly with pain. His mouth was full of sand and blood and his head rocked to a vicious kick.

Then he heard a booming shout: "Hatali Kintiel."

The kicks stopped. It was the name that did it. Kintiel. Rim heard the shuffling of feet around him, the hoarse breathing. He spat blood and sand, rolled over, and got to one knee. He saw that they were spreading away from him, slowly, reluctantly, their faces flushed with anger and frustration. Standing Waters was the last to move, his bronze chest gleaming with sweat, his black eyes glittering.

The solid ranks parted as the Indians turned to face the other way, slowly separating to leave a pathway that led to Rim. And through that pathway, Rim could see Kintiel. He was alone with the *yei* blanket held in deep folds about his broad shoulders. None of the sly humor was left in his lithic face; it was stern and forbidding. In his rolling, bear-like gait he walked down the path in the crowd till he stood above Rim. He spoke in Spanish.

"What are you doing down here?"

Rim got to his feet, swaying dizzily. He waved his arm at the hogan. "The white woman. She's in there."

Kintiel glanced at the hogan, then at Standing Waters. "So be it," he said. "Standing Waters has chosen her as his squaw, his slave."

"You'll get her out."

"I cannot."

Rim was silent a moment. This was like a grim game of mental chess. One wrong move on his part and Sherry would be forfeit. He looked at the brooding, stony face of the *hatali* and felt a little awed by the incisive power of the savage mind he opposed. Yet he sensed now that Kintiel had brought him here for a purpose. And it must be a purpose of deep significance to Kintiel, to make him oppose the will of the warriors in saving Rim's life.

Rim knew the risk he was taking. But he had to go on that assumption, had to take the chance that the medicine man would go a step farther.

"For years I have heard of your power," Rim told the man. "And now I have seen the fear and awe with which your people look upon you. I think you can get this woman for me."

"And if I cannot?"

"I'll do it."

"They will kill you."

"Then you'll lose me, won't you?"

Kintiel looked into Rim's face for a long time. Finally a smile of grudging admiration touched his lips. "I believe you would, too." He paused, his face growing dark and somber. Then he turned to Standing Waters. He swept aside his robe and gestured majestically toward the dwelling. Then he launched into a long oration. Rim could understand but part of it. Kintiel seemed to be telling the headman that this was for the good of all their people, that Standing Waters had no right to jeopardize the safety of the whole tribe over the possession of one woman, that he would be nobler swallowing his pride and giving her up than he would be in fighting for her. When Kintiel was finished, Standing Waters answered harshly.

"*Do-tah.*"

Kintiel looked over his shoulder at Rim. "Do you understand?"

"He said no."

"I can do no more, *Belinkana.* Standing Waters is the war chief of all the clans in the canyon."

"I do not think you have exerted your power."

"I have done all I can."

Rim knew it was still the chess game, and this was the crucial move. "Then it's up to me," he said. He started walking toward the hogan. A sighing sound rose from the assembled Indians, like the moaning of a distant wind; then it became a sullen mutter, and their ranks began to shift and stir. Standing Waters pulled his knife. Rim was two feet from the hogan.

"*Belinkana!*"

It came from Kintiel, sharp, commanding. Rim stopped. The sound of the crowd stopped. Standing Waters leaned forward, waiting to lunge. They were all waiting, their eyes on Kintiel like bright beads, a savage hope of vindication in their faces. Solemnly Kintiel walked to Rim. His face was bleak with anger.

"You are a *tchindi*," he said. "But you are also a brave man. And now you will need all your courage. If we do not succeed, your death will be more unspeakable than you can imagine. Follow me."

He stooped through the door. Rim glanced back, then followed. The other Indians crowded in. Sherry was still sitting on the pelts against the wall. She had pulled her hair back from her eyes and was staring at the scene, naked and in dazed fright. Rim went to her immediately, kneeling beside her, taking her hands.

"Sherry, we're going to get you out of this."

She stared blankly at him, as if not knowing him. Then recognition began to creep through the glazed surface of her eyes. He saw intense shame fill them then and she turned aside from him, the dirty, matted hair falling over her face once more.

"Sherry," he said, "we're here to help you."

But she would not turn back. In her averted face, in the whole rigid tension of her body, he could see the humiliation and outrage she had suffered. He was helpless to do more. Holding her hands reassuringly, he turned to watch Kintiel.

The hogan was packed now. The rear ranks were standing against the wall, the low roof forcing them to bow their heads. The front ranks were squatting on their haunches. Kintiel had hunkered down by the fire, thus leaving a small spot in front of Sherry open. Gontzo had managed to squeeze in beside Rim, trembling and frowning and working his mouth.

"Kintiel will make a sand painting," he told Rim. "The gods will tell him what to do."

It was a bizarre scene, with the flickering fire casting its uncertain light across the coppery bodies, the glittering eyes, the sullen, primitive faces. Standing Waters knelt in the front ranks, watching Kintiel suspiciously. There was something childish in their intentness. It took away their savagery for a moment, their ominous threat.

Then Kintiel picked up a handful of ashes from the edge of the fire. A sigh went up from the crowd. Gontzo moaned.

"*Do-tah,*" he said. "*Do-tah.* You cannot do that."

"What is it?" Rim asked.

"He is using ashes for the painting instead of sand," Gontzo said. "It is witchcraft." The old man was so perturbed that he did not revert back to Navajo as he pleaded with Kintiel. "You cannot do that. You cannot reveal yourself. They will kill you!"

Kintiel looked over his shoulder. His lips were spread in a crafty smile and his black eyes twinkled sardonically. "They have long been calling me a witch," he told Gontzo. "Perhaps it is time for proof."

"But they will throw you off the cliff."

"The test has to come some time. We will see now who has the power."

With a practiced movement he spread the ashes on the hard-packed floor. Another sigh went up and the men pressed farther away. Only Standing

Waters remained where he had sat. There was a look of ugly triumph in his face. He said something so swiftly that Rim could not follow. He looked to Gontzo for translation. The old man quavered: "Standing Waters says he has been waiting for this moment for a long time. Kintiel has doomed himself."

With quick, deft touches, Kintiel was forming a figure out of the ashes on the floor. Rim saw the expression on Standing Waters's face begin to grow taut, fixed. The man started edging away, his eyes held with growing apprehension on the ash painting.

"Now the spirits will come down to see," Gontzo moaned. "Only they will not be good spirits."

Kintiel finished, looking up at Standing Waters. The only sound was of breathing, all of their breathing, like the sigh of a vast sea. Sweat gathered on Rim's brow. Even Sherry was looking now, dazedly, uncomprehendingly. Then Kintiel pointed his finger at Standing Waters.

"The painting is of Standing Waters," Gontzo said.

Rim saw Standing Waters's thick lips part, saw fear come into his face. Then, with an outraged sound, he started to rise, started to pull that knife again.

"*Oh, tchindis!*" Kintiel's voice rang out like the toll of a great bell. He threw up his arms, looking at the roof. "*Oh, Anaye, oh, Yeitso,* look down upon this act tonight." The words stopped Standing Waters, it checked the whole forward surge of the ranks. Kintiel went on with his oration. Rim could understand words and phrases, and could piece the rest together. "Look down upon this act tonight and remember it forevermore until the one upon which it is performed is no longer a man. Put the spirit of the bear into him so that when he rides his saddle will be empty, when he walks there will be no sound of his moccasins, when he speaks there will be no words in his mouth. Blind him as a man whose eyes have been picked out by the crows. Make him silent as the wind that cannot blow. Turn his spawn to coyotes and his squaws to snakes and let his blood become as the milk of the goat."

From a rawhide pouch at his waist Kintiel pulled a miniature bow. Standing Waters's eyes began to shine. He stared at the bow like a man hypnotized. A moan rose from the crowd. With a strip of rawhide, Kintiel strung the bow. Then he laid it on the ground, a foot away from the figure formed by the ashes. And upon the rawhide string he placed a bead of jet-black cannel coal.

They all stared at the bow, mesmerized. The bead seemed to be moving on the string. Rim could not believe his eyes. The gut was humming and jumping as if trying to keep the bead from leaping at the painting of ashes. The cords in Standing Waters's neck stretched the skin. A strained mewing sound left his slack lips. Kintiel seemed lost in a trance. His body swayed.

"Strike him with the bead, give him pain where it hits, and let the pain spread over his whole body and fill him with dreams of bear and of *tchindi*. Strike him with the bead!"

The bit of cannel coal leaped from the bowstring and struck the ashen figure. Standing Waters emitted a sickening grunt, as if he himself had been struck. He stared blankly at the bead, lying on the ashen figure. Then he broke into a wild howl. Yelping, shouting, screaming, he jumped to his feet, trying to get through the crowd.

He threw himself against them like a mad thing, unable to get through the press. The hogan was a bedlam. All of the Indians were on their feet, fighting and kicking in a wild effort to get through the door. They jammed up there and three of them fell to their knees. Shouting wildly, Standing Waters tore his way through, followed by others, trampling their fellows. Rim pushed himself across in front of Sherry as the struggling mass battered him back and forth. Finally the room was emptied. Even Gontzo was gone. Outside, Rim could hear the shouting and calling spread throughout the whole village, the echoes striking the walls of the canyon and multiplying into a hollow, booming din.

Kintiel still sat on the floor. His head was sunk on his chest and his great shoulders were bowed and he stared with empty eyes at the bow, the bead, the ashen figure. He seemed completely spent. Rim felt drained himself, emotionally and physically. He had witnessed something not often revealed to civilized man, a moment out of humanity's dark past.

At last Kintiel raised his head, looking

around the room, finally at Rim. "You have your woman now," he said. "Cover her. We must return to the witch house."

Chapter Fourteen

It took them a long time to get Sherry up the narrow, treacherous trail. She leaned heavily against Rim, but she would not look at him. Below, they could see the tiny figures of the Bead Clan running back and forth through the village, crossing the river, gathering in knots by the cornfields. The people of other clans had heard of the witchcraft and were now coming into view from their villages, long lines of them that joined the Bead Clan and covered the floor of the canyon till they looked like a swarm of ants.

They got Sherry into one of the cliff houses, where two of Kintiel's wives were mixing cedar ashes with meal to make their blue paper bread. They were both young women, clothed in black dresses, blue-bordered and red-tasseled.

They showed Sherry a genuine concern, clucking and murmuring over her as they escorted her off to the side, helped her into a calico skirt and deer-skin top chosen from among their own wardrobe. She seemed indifferent to the clothes just as she seemed unashamed for others to see her in her nakedness. The women brought Sherry back to sit on a heap of robes against the wall. Rim approached her, going to one knee before where she was seated, and took her hand.

"Sherry," he said. She turned her head away. He spoke more softly. "It's all right now. I want to help you."

She did not answer. He saw soundless tears tracing silvery tracks in the grime of her face. She absolutely would not turn to look at him.

"It will take time," Kintiel said. "My women will take care of her. They will make tea for her and wash her and feed her. Then she can rest."

Rim was reluctant to leave her, but he saw that shame and shock walled her off from him. At least she was safe now. He rose and went to the door. He stopped there to look back. Her face was still averted.

Kintiel was waiting for Rim outside. He led the way up the trail, past other caves, to the mesa top above. Here, looking broodingly upon his people swarming so far below, he said: "I have done what you asked."

"I wish her complete freedom."

"Then you will do what I ask?"

"If I can, and it does not betray my people, I will."

Kintiel was silent for a while. Then, "When you go, she will go with you."

"And when will that be?"

"I will answer you this way." Kintiel looked into the canyon again. "Every man down there has nothing but hate in his heart for your people. They want nothing with the white man but war. They want nothing for them but death. From the beginning, I have raised my voice against it. I have said that unless we find peace with the white man we will destroy ourselves. And the time of that destruction is perilously near."

"The white man has a different picture of you," Rim said. "He thinks you're behind every raid, every scalping, every massacre."

Kintiel looked at Rim, almost sadly. "Will the white man ever know the truth about the Navajo?"

"Perhaps some white men," Rim said. "I know of those who agree with you, who would like to gain peace without further bloodshed. Kit Carson is one. Though he fights you, it hurts him in his heart."

"But there are some who wish the fighting to go on. Among them the gray suits you call Confederates. More than anything else, it is their guns and their lies spread among my people that have kept us at war."

"You spoke of the spy, the one who was sent by the Confederates to accomplish this. If he could be reached, would it stop their work?"

Kintiel nodded. "He is the key. Without his leadership, the rest of the group would fall apart."

"And you still claim you don't know who he is?"

"I swear by the *yei*. I would give my life to know. I believe that his destruction would save my people. I sent Peshlikai out to hunt him. That was before Carson began his campaign, and friendly Navajos could move among you. Peshlikai failed. But he sent me word of another man, the only one among all the whites who seemed to believe as I believed, who sought to expose the traitors among his people, who could help us, if he would. That man was you."

"Then it was Peshlikai following me that night in Tucson?"

"I told him to bring you here," Kintiel said. "But he was captured before he could do so. The raid on your wagon train gave him another chance. I cannot send him out again, *Belinkana*. I could not even go myself. All who left this canyon would be captured."

"So you seek one who can move freely among the whites."

Kintiel looked into his eyes. "That is what I seek."

Rim had sensed something like this, since their talk the night before. The full revelation of Kintiel's purpose in bringing him here was staggering. Yet, ironically, how closely it paralleled what Rim had been seeking since his return from the war!

But suspicion remained. After all the harrowing legends Rim had heard of this man, it was hard to accept him in the present light as a lonely, threatened outcast, ostracized from his people because he had sought peace when they sought war.

Sometimes he seemed capable of such

nobility. Rim had seen him when he seemed all Indian, primitive, superstitious, spiritual, capable of much sacrifice for his people. But his other side seemed to mock those things — the slyness, the sophistication, the cynicism. It must have been a trick, the business with the bead and the bow. Could a man stoop to such fakery and still believe in his gods? The *yei* blanket was another symbol of his mockery. The *yei* were the gods, and only the medicine men had a right to depict them in the sand paintings. The weaver who had dared the evil power of the gods to make this blanket would probably never be known. But in wearing it, Kintiel defied the most deeply rooted superstitions of his people, and announced his own malignant cynicism in doing so.

Kintiel saw his suspicion and wrapped the blanket closely about his great shoulders. "You do not trust me completely yet, *Belinkana,* and neither do I trust you. I have asked the gods. They have not spoken."

"What would make them answer?"

Kintiel's eyes grew piercing. "Do you laugh at our gods?"

"My father always told me it was more childish to laugh at a people's gods than to believe in them."

"Your father was a wise man. So, perhaps, are you." Kintiel brooded a moment longer, then turned abruptly down the trail without looking again at Rim.

Thoughtfully, Rim followed.

Late that night, in the shadow of Spider Rock, the Bead Clan held a fire dance. All eyes were so intent on the dance that few noticed Rim's presence as he moved closer, accompanied by Gontzo. The fire had burned low and the Turn-to-White Dance, which had begun the nocturnal vigil, had concluded long before. A medicine man — Gontzo told Rim his name was Adakhai — announced the beginning of this ultimate ceremony by blowing a shrill whistle repeatedly.

There was a large corral nearby and it was here that the twelve dancers had been spraying each other's naked bodies, painting themselves white to susurrated guttural sounds of what sounded to Rim like *"Prrr!"* and *"Eh-yah'!"* Their preparations concluded, the dancers now filed before the fire on which new logs had been piled in great quantity and which now roared, shooting sparks and flames high into the air, almost to the top of Spider Rock itself. Each dancer held a cedar-bark torch, about four feet long and burning brightly.

Dancing around the raging fire, the twelve waved their torches toward it and chanted. Gontzo whispered in Spanish the meaning of the words. The song was repeated again and again, as if endless.

> *The first time they came*
> *out of the earth!*
> *Hostudi!*
> *The torch they put on me*
> *does not injure me.*
> *The torch they put on me*
> *does not injure me.*
> *Rather, I am holy with it*

Hostudi, Gontzo explained briefly, was Little Sleepy Owl, he who had first created the Big Fire Dance. The chanted verse changed and altered, but always it meant the same thing. The dancers, Gontzo said, were protected from the fire because they believed.

But it does me no harm
I am holy with the fire.

The leader of the dancers then ignited a bundle of bark and, as it burst into flames, cast it over the corral to the east. In time three more bundles were similarly ignited and thrown to the other directions, to the south, to the north, and to the west. The People began breathing into their hands and then gestured as if casting their breath away from them. They were casting off sickness.

Then, the twelve, with their burning torches, began a wild race around the fire, beating each other over the back with the blazing cedar bark to loud, continued cries in the night of *"Prrr!"* Faster and faster they ran, fanning their torches until they were a long flame. It was as if the *tchindis* themselves took possession of the dancers. They became demons, pirouetting and capering before The People, their nude bodies now in a frenzy, breaking away suddenly to thrust out the torch to burn a rival dancer, to set him on fire.

The pace increased. The velocity became so rapid Rim could scarcely follow all the movements of the dancers when, suddenly, singly they dashed directly into the raging fire, dancing with immunity on the beds of red coals that surrounded the conflagration. They scattered the coals and trampled them. Their naked bodies, agleam with sweat and the white paint, shone, bathed in flames. Battles now would break out between individual dancers, one jumping the other, until unexpectedly they dashed out of the circle of flames into the dark night, beating at each other's backs and buttocks with the flaring torches.

Daylight was stealing gently over the canyon walls. The smoldering coals were quenched and the big corral was now broken in three more places so that there were four gates, instead of one.

"You should have brought your woman," Gontzo said to Rim as they paced quietly back to the narrow trail leading up to the caves. "The fire dance can purify the soul. It has ever been thus since the time of *Hostudi*."

Rim did not answer, so awed and overcome with emotion did he find himself. A great quiet had descended into his soul for the first time since he had returned from the war.

It was as if Gontzo understood. He said no more.

Late that same afternoon, rested now and still strangely at peace, Rim followed the trail to the cliff house where Sherry was being kept. One of Kintiel's wives was weaving in the corner. When Rim entered, she discreetly left.

Sherry sat on a robe against the far wall. She was clean again. Her own clothes had been washed and mended and she was wearing them. Her cheeks had a freshly scrubbed look and her hair had been combed out and drawn behind her head and tied with a blue *banda.* Yet the misery was still in her face, as she raised her eyes briefly to Rim, and then looked at the floor again.

He knew what this represented to her. It was the culmination, a final, terrible justification of her hatred for this country. In her eyes, this land and its people could have done nothing worse, short of death, to her. If there had ever been any hope left that she could accept the land, it was gone now. He was suddenly filled with pity for her, and a sense of defeat and depression as deep as hers stole in upon him, replacing the tranquillity he had known since the fire dance. He sat beside her.

"Feel better?"

She nodded.

"Anything I can do?"

She turned her head farther aside and her hands sought each other in her lap, something desperate in the way they locked together. "Rim, please — it isn't that I don't want to see you — but can't you see . . . ?"

"You have nothing to be ashamed of, Sherry."

She put her hands abruptly to her face, covering it, bowing her shoulders. She made a choked, sobbing sound. "I can't help it."

Anger swept him. He had tried tenderness, repeatedly, and had got nowhere. He had to reach her somehow. He tried to make his voice gentle.

"Look. Maybe what happened to you is a terrible thing. But it's happened to other women and they've pulled through it. Under any circumstances, it's over now. You've got to go on. And from here on out, it's not what it did to your body that matters. It's what it did to your soul. If you can face it, and go on from there, it won't hurt you."

Her sobbing had stopped. She remained bent over, hands to her face, but he saw her take a ragged breath, and knew she meant to speak. Finally her voice came, rusty, strained.

"How can I face it? How can I face you? How can you come here like this, knowing what happened?"

He put a hand on her arm. "Sherry, it doesn't matter to me. Can't you understand that? It doesn't change my feeling for you. I loved you in Tucson, fool that I was back then about everything else, and I love you now, and I want to help you. Whether you go back to New England or not, I want to help you. If you let this defeat you, you'll lock yourself up in some dark room. You'll let this twist you and ruin the rest of your life. You'll be stiff, sour, dried-up by one calamity, jumping at your own shadow, afraid of men, afraid of life. I have seen men maimed and ruined by the war the same way. You can't let that happen."

He saw her shoulders pull together, saw her whole body seem to shrink. For a moment he knew doubt. Was he being needlessly cruel? Had he gone too far? Then impatience swept him. He had to go on.

"I don't think you're that way, Sherry. Inside, you've got courage. I've seen it more than once. We might have been killed in that runaway wagon. You wouldn't jump. You stayed with me and you weren't afraid. I saw it, Sherry. Real, honest emotion, with guts to it. Emotion that you've been trying to hide from all your life. Let it out now, Sherry. Be a woman, be honest with yourself. What's happened is bad. To a woman like you, I guess the only thing worse these people could have done was tor- ture you, or kill you. And yet, how much did it really hurt you?"

She turned farther away, making a choked sound. He squeezed her arm.

"Sherry, I'm not trying to make light of it. I'm only trying to show you how it is. You're still alive. You've still got a man who loves you, and we're getting out of here, I promise you. Remember Steve Swan? He had lost an arm in the war. Did that stop him? He was as good as any man with two arms and better than most. He didn't brood about it. He was alive and he had the future."

Slowly her hands slid from her face to her lap. She was crying no longer. But she was still turned so that her back was to him, and her voice sounded tight as a bowstring at its breaking point.

"Rim, I can't talk about it. Please leave me, I beg of you."

His shoulders bowed and the lines of his bearded face deepened. He wanted so much to help her, and he could do nothing. Finally he rose and, silently, went out.

Chapter Fifteen

October was gone now. The back-to-back month was gone, white on top and green on the bottom. And November was over, the month of light winds, and December, the month of big winds. It was the month of snow, of the big crust, with the snows borne in on a howling gale and the river frozen over, and the Navajos huddling miserably around their fires in their hogans. There was not enough food within Chelly to support the people through the winter and hunting parties risked capture and death by traveling in an ever widening circle outside the canyon.

The news they brought back was frightening. Kit Carson was closing in. His regiment of volunteers had entirely destroyed the crops and the villages of the Indians outside the canyon. Starving, facing a winter without food or shelter, thousands of Navajos had surrendered and were beginning the long walk to Fort Sumner. The only real hold-outs left were those wild clans within the Navajo stronghold, Canyon de Chelly. Standing Waters bragged that he had no fear. The canyon was impregnable. In two centuries no white invader had been able to take it.

Rim made his way down the icy canyon trail. Its mouth opened onto Canyon de Chelly. He had been avoiding the villages on the floor in his walks, but it was cold today and Rim sought the shortest route to his cave. The few times he had approached Indians, they had avoided him like the plague, and he had faith in the immunity Kintiel's witchcraft gave him. He headed boldly up the banks of the frozen river, crossing the canyon near the village of the Bead Clan. He was aware that Horse Girl was trailing him at a distance.

On the fringe of the hogans he saw a figure sitting cross-legged under a brush arbor. The man was bent over a crude bellows but, when he saw Rim, he sat straight. It was Peshlikai.

"Ahalani, Belinkana," he said. *"Greetings, white man."*

"Ahalani, Peshlikai."

"You have been to the sweat lodge again?"

"I just came from it."

"Standing Waters goes there, too, these days to purify himself. He fasts and sings *hozhoni* songs and has the *hatalis* make sand paintings to drive out the spirit of the bear. But nothing will avail. He sickens and soon will die."

Rim did not answer. Peshlikai bent his narrow hatchet face over the bellows.

"Is it not dangerous for one of Kintiel's men to be down here?" Rim asked.

"Kintiel has given orders that you not be harmed."

"I speak of you," Rim said.

"I belong to the Bead Clan. Standing Waters is my uncle."

"Kintiel gave me to believe that you were his man. He sent you out to find the Confederate spy."

"When a colt grows up, he runs alone," Peshlikai said. He dropped a Mexican silver dollar into the pottery crucible, pumping the cottonwood arms of the bellows. They closed the bag like an accordion, ejecting air through the nozzle. The fire beneath the crucible leaped high and the dollar began to melt. Rim had to speak louder, over the hoarse puff of the bellows.

"Have you ceased to believe the Confederates are keeping you at war?"

"Perhaps the gray suits are right. Standing Waters says war is our only salvation."

"And you have renounced Kintiel for that?"

Peshlikai lifted the crucible with a pair of wood tongs, pouring the melted silver into a sandstone mold, cut into the form of a horse. "How can a man truly want to save his people, when he allies himself with the enemy?" he asked.

"Perhaps I am not an enemy," Rim said.

"You walk with too many shadows to be a friend."

"You speak in riddles again."

"The gods speak in riddles, yet they speak truth."

"And those shadows?"

Peshlikai looked up at Rim. That smokiness was in his eyes, robbing them of their bead-blankness. "Do you know our *Hlin Blyin?*"

"The Song of the Horse?"

"Do not listen too closely, *Belinkana.*"

Rim looked back through the hogans. Horse Girl was no longer following him. She was not in sight.

During the following days, Sherry showed little change. Her shame and humiliation did not seem so intense, but there was still a great distance between them whenever Rim visited her. Despite the cruel weather, Rim's impatience was becoming almost unbearable. He could not understand why he was being kept here so long and Kintiel's explanation, that he was waiting for a favorable sign from the gods, failed to satisfy him. His impatience renewed thoughts of escape that had come to him during his early imprisonment here. One day he eluded Gontzo and went to the rim of the canyon, making his way westward across the icy, wind-swept plateau. They had given him a man's blue shirt of rough wool and over this he wore a heavy coat, but still he was cold.

He did not know how many precarious, wearying miles he traveled before he came to the end of the canyon. From this height he could see miles across the desert. There were the gargantuan playing blocks of the mesas strewn across a carpet whose warp was the endless stretch of buckskin sand, whose woof was the olive blur of grease-wood. Beyond that, in the vast and hazy distance, stretched a band of mountains, something so rich about their damask texture that he felt the distinct impulse to reach out and touch them.

He saw how hopeless was the thought of escape. A horse could not be taken out over the plateau; the only exit from the canyon was on its floor, directly through the sentinels placed at the mouth. He could see their ant-like figures crouched in the rocks or moving from vantage point to vantage point. It would be impossible to get by them, even at night.

Finally he turned to make his way back. On the rim of the canyon he saw a figure. It was Horse Girl. Over her blue velvet tunic she wore a heavy, red blanket, slit in the center so it could be worn like a poncho. She held it tightly about her slim shoulders, but its corners fluttered like aspen leaves in the chill wind.

"Why do you follow me?" he asked in Spanish. She did not answer. He approached her slowly. He saw her slim body draw up, like a doe poised for flight. He stopped. "Are you afraid of me?" he asked. He had come to expect no answer. He thought she would wheel and go in the next moment, as she had always done before. But she didn't move. Her lips had taken on a surprising fullness for such a small and delicate face, giving her a pensive look.

"I was once afraid," she said.

Her words took him completely off guard. They seemed to break the eerie spell that had always been cast over their meetings by her silence.

"Is that why you did not tell the truth about Yaki Peters?" Rim asked.

"I thought you no different from him. I am sorry now." Her Spanish was not so fluent as Peshlikai's or Kintiel's. She spoke it in a halting, hesitant voice, frowning over some of the unfamiliar words. It made her seem like a little girl learning the alphabet. He smiled and moved closer.

"Why have you been silent?"

Her eyes lowered. She did not answer. He was but three feet away now. He stopped.

"Horse Girl," he said. "How did you get the name?"

She turned her eyes toward the sun, a pale disk in the west. "*Johano-ai* is the sun god. Each day from his hogan in the east he rides across the skies to his hogan in the west. Today he rides his turquoise horse. When the heavens are dark with storm, he rides his horse of cannel coal." As she spoke, her shyness dropped away. Her cheeks began to shine and her eyes kindled with little lights. "The galloping horse of *Johano-ai* raises not dust but *pitistchi,* glittering grains of the sacred pollen that we use in our ceremonies. You can see it today." She pointed to the horizon and he saw the delicate, golden mist of great distance joining sky and earth. "When I was born," she said, "the turquoise horse covered the edge of the world with *pitistchi.* My people said it was a good omen and named me Horse Girl."

The simple beauty of the story, the wonderful child-like faith shining in her eyes, seemed to strip all the sophistries and cynicism of civilization from him. For a moment he was not modern man, seeking logic and reason and proof. He was as close to the earth and the sky as she.

Then he remembered what Peshlikai had said about the Song of the Horse. "Do not listen too closely, *Belinkana.*"

He looked at Horse Girl, and the full impact of Peshlikai's warning struck him. Then he realized that she was no longer looking at the sky, but was studying his face carefully.

"You do not laugh at our gods?"

"Perhaps I believe."

She took a step closer. "Few white men do."

"They also have stories that are but symbols of the truth. Perhaps they do not stop to think of this."

Her voice was barely audible. "You are strange."

"Is that why you follow me?"

Her eyes lowered again, and a delicate flush tinted her face. He took another step. It was the closest he had ever been to her. There was a smell of wildness to her, musky, feral, untamed — the scent of primitive caves and of clean, pungent dust swept across endless wastes and of brief-blooming desert flowers that die when a man touches them.

"It is the time for truth," he said. "Did Kintiel set you to watch me, as Peshlikai was watching me in Tucson?"

Her head came up and anger made a bright flash in her eyes. For a moment all the shyness was gone from her and she spoke with a brittle intensity that surprised him.

"That is not so. I come of my own will." She stopped, surprised at her own boldness.

He said, "And why do you come?"

"We haven't had much time together," she said.

"And yet you're going to marry Peshlikai."

She pouted in a sudden irritation. "He is very handsome."

"Do you love him?"

She tossed her head. "They say he makes love with great skill."

"Do you love him?" he insisted, pushed into making an issue of this by some indefinable emotion within him, which had been growing since his first sight of her. The evasion of all that coquetry had left her now, and the candid tone of her voice surprised him.

"What is love?" she asked.

"This," he said, and didn't have to move far to get his arm about her, bending her head back in the kiss. All the budding promise of those lips bloomed beneath his, ripened, with thought blotted from mind, leaving only a myriad of dim sensations, of his weight bearing against her, of her fingers digging into his back for a moment in her first startled denial, and then relaxing for another moment that became an instant of complete surrender. Then she pushed him away, spinning from him to stand, panting, staring up at him. Neither of them spoke for a long space, and he watched all the mingled anger and surprise and puzzlement in her eyes focus into one dominant expression. He tried to read in it the same intense attraction he felt for her.

Suddenly he realized the betrayal this was. He held out his hand. "Look," he said, haltingly. "Forget it. We . . . I shouldn't have done it. I'm a dirty heel. I have no right. . . ."

"Maybe it goes beyond right," she said, still staring at him with that shining wonder in her eyes. "Why did you do it?"

"I can't explain," he said. "It was just in me, that's all. You just drew me. Ever since I first saw you. Like no other woman ever has."

"That's what I mean," she said, in a soft, husky voice, as if surprised at her own boldness. "When something drives you that much, you don't stop to think of right or wrong. Is that what love is? It is good. You couldn't have shown me so well with a million words."

Some vague mockery had entered her voice, and he spoke roughly. "I told you to forget it."

She touched her lips. "Maybe I can't forget it."

He stared at her in a twisted way, unable to understand the emotions in himself now, unable to believe that this deep sense of betrayal had not completely blotted out the intense attraction she held for him. And yet it hadn't. The attraction was still there, as strong, as impelling as ever. His eyes rested on that pulsing, brown throat.

She moistened her lips. "Do you have love for the white woman?"

He wondered why he hesitated. At last, with a reluctance he did not understand, he said, "Yes."

She stared at him a moment with wide, luminous eyes. Her hands fluttered like copper birds, then settled against the edges of her blanket, gripping it tightly. At last, without a word, she turned and left.

He stood there watching her figure grow smaller and smaller, until it was completely out of sight. The wind whipped across the chill plateau and filled the world with loneliness.

He made his way back across the mesa, through the broken, rocky plateau, toward the trail. He was within sight of the rim when he heard the sound. At first he thought it was gravel skittering off the edge before the wind. Then it gained identity. There was something musical about it. Tinkling. Jangling.

He stopped, his back against a wall of broken, tumbled rock. For a while all he could hear was the sad plaint of the wind. Then it came again, the barbaric jangle of silver bracelets.

Sweat came to his face, cold and clammy. He knew what it meant. It could have no other significance. There was no doubt in his mind. He looked at his hands, his bare, empty hands.

The jangling came again, closer this time. The very insolence of it infuriated him. Another man, doing this, would have removed the bracelets. But Peshlikai, arrogant in the knowledge of Rim's helplessness, had not even bothered. Perhaps he even wanted Rim to sweat a little, to suffer a little, before the game was finished.

The sound came once more. It seemed to be at his right. He tried to move away from the sound. Night was coming swiftly and the broken plateau was filled with pockets of smoky shadow. He made his way through a tumbled heap of rocks. Getting down into a gully, he started a miniature avalanche. Stones rattled and clattered to the bottom.

He crouched halfway down the slope, cursing himself for his stupidity. Then the jangling came again. He got down into the gully without trying to hide his noise; the pressure of that jangling at his back filled him with the impulse to run. It took a great effort of will to hold himself back. If he could keep it up till night, he might have a chance. It wasn't long now. Then the tinkling again, closer.

He stopped at the head of the gully, looking out on a sand flat without cover. It stretched clear to the rim of the canyon and there wasn't even a bush to hide him. He had run himself into a trap.

The sound came again, behind, above.

He could not turn back. And he could not leave the gully without being completely exposed. The blood was pounding in his temples. His palms were sweating. That's what you want, isn't it? His gaunt, black Irish face twisted with anger. "Do not listen too closely, *Belinkana.*" Well he had listened. How else could it be?

Closer now, closer than ever. Like Christmas bells on a mule hitch. Almost above. He lay flat against the steep slope of the gully. He thought of Sherry and knew poignant regret, then anger again. Fear and anger and regret all mixed up, making him sweat, making the blood so thick in his throat he could hardly breathe. He twisted his head around till he saw a rock. He slid over and reached out and took it in his hand. The tinkle. The jangle. Right above him. His head turned up. His eyes bulged like a frog's with the strained position.

There was a grunt, a sudden discordant jangle louder than ever before. His hand tightened spasmodically around the rock and his whole body went rigid.

Nothing came. All he could hear was the wind now. Like a lost soul it roamed around on the plateau above him, whining softly, rising, dying, leaving a moment of utter silence. The breath was blocked up in him and the pressure was like a great weight compressing his whole body. Then a new sound came. A sobbing, like a little child's, muffled, hoarse, hopeless sobbing. It did not rise or fall, become less or more; it just went on in that utter hopelessness.

Finally he could stand it no longer. He slid down into the gully and worked back through its bottom for a hundred yards. Then he crawled to the lip, gripping the rock so tightly his fingers hurt.

Peshlikai lay sprawled on the ground, three feet from the edge of the gully where Rim had been before. Beneath the Indian lay his rifle. In his back, buried to the hilt, was the knife.

And crouched over him, her back to Rim, her face hidden in her hands, still sobbing that way, was Horse Girl.

Chapter Sixteen

If a man marries into his mother's clan, he will go crazy and jump into the fire. Black paint on the body will prevent *tchindis* from entering it. Devils and witches always turn left upon entering a door. Hatali Kintiel came into the cave room and turned left and seated himself cross-legged before the fire. He looked at Rim and Horse Girl a long moment. Then he said: "Gontzo told me. How did it happen?"

"Peshlikai was going to kill me," Rim said.

"I have seen it coming," Kintiel answered. "His jealousy was a rat gnawing at his belly."

There was a damp, cold silence in the cave. Horse Girl sat like a wooden thing, staring into the snapping blaze of the meager fire. Kintiel's squaws had seen Rim returning down the trail with her. After sending Gontzo for Kintiel, they had insisted on taking her into their quarters. But all their murmured consolation and old hen clucking would not break through her silence. She seemed appalled by what she had done, seemed dazed by the enormity of it. Sherry sat on a folded blanket at the rear of the cave. She was watching Horse Girl intently.

"The gods have spoken," Kintiel said.

Rim frowned at him. "What?"

"Horse Girl is their instrument. They would not have kept you alive had they not wanted me to use you. It is time." He paused, studying Rim. Then he said, "I can tell you things now that I could not trust with you before. Standing Waters thinks we can hold our stronghold against Carson. I do not."

"Then you should be glad. If Carson wins, there will be peace."

"Do you think the Confederatcs will give up that easily?" Kintiel said. "Here is one of the things I could not tell you before. We did not get all the guns from your wagon train. We got only three wagons."

Rim could not help looking at Sherry. She had a meager knowledge of Spanish and had caught enough of the words to realize what Kintiel had said. She shook her head, meeting Rim's eyes for a moment, then looking at the floor. "I don't know, Rim," she murmured. "It might be true."

"I think it was planned that way from the beginning," Kintiel said. "No war party from Chelly would be big enough to take a train that size. In cutting out three wagons, we got more than we hoped for. And I think the Confederates got what they hoped for. Every soldier of the escort was killed."

"You're saying Yaki Peters is a Confederate?" Rim asked.

Kintiel nodded. "And his mule skinners, handpicked for this trip. As you know, half the men in Tucson were sympathizers with the gray suits."

Rim wanted it very clear now. "And Yaki wanted to get rid of that military escort?"

"How else could he take the wagons where he wanted?" Kintiel said.

"But if the Confederates wanted you to have the guns, why not let your war party take them all?"

"Because it was not the plan to give the few clans in this canyon all those guns. In the three wagons we captured were enough arms for us."

"What was the plan?" Rim asked.

Kintiel bent toward him. "The Navajos who have surrendered are going to be sent to *Hwalte,* which you call Fort Sumner. Some of them have already started the long walk. But many of them are still being held at Fort Wingate. The bulk of the tribe is there now, thousands of them. Carson has but a few hundred soldiers to guard them. What do you think would happen if those Navajos were armed?"

Rim felt the muscles bunch along his bearded jaw as he realized what Kintiel meant. The expression on his face was answer enough for the Indian.

"It would be the worst massacre this country has ever seen," Kintiel said. "It would be a crushing defeat to your people. It would set my whole nation free again, armed as they have never been armed before."

Rim was silent a moment, awed by the boldness of such a plan. Then he shook his head. "But where are the wagons now? It's hard to hide a train that size."

"Who can hunt for them? Carson is busy with his campaign. He needs every man. And none of us can leave Chelly without being captured. It is my belief that this is the goal for which the Confederates have worked, from the beginning. A final blow that would break the white man's grip on this land for good."

Rim looked at him, growing angry. "And you could wait, could hold me here, knowing that?"

"If they had meant to strike at once, those guns would have reached the Navajos at Wingate long ago," Kintiel said. "The fact that they did not convinces me that the gray suits are waiting to see what happens here. If Carson takes Chelly, hundreds of our wildest warriors would be added to the fighting men already at Fort Wingate. Arm them all and Carson would be overwhelmed." There was silence in the cave save for the snap of a dying fire. Then Kintiel looked at Rim and spoke again. "You must find those guns, *Belinkana.* You must stop this thing from happening."

Rim did not answer. It was a bizarre responsibility, hard to believe. Yet he was too intimately concerned with the nebulous pattern of all the things that had led up to this culmination. It was like a steadily growing pressure against him.

Then they heard someone stumbling

up the trail outside, and Gontzo's shrill voice. *"Ahdilohee, Ahdilohee!"*

Kintiel looked at Rim, his face growing so taut that the cheekbones looked sharp as arrowheads, thrusting against the ruddy flesh. And they heard the first shots, like the distant sputter of a wind-blown fire, multiplied and magnified by the sounding walls of the canyon, till they were like a whole battery of cannon booming right in the cave room. Over the frightening sound, Rim heard Kintiel's single word. "Carson."

Rim was already on his feet. He was the first through the door, followed by Kintiel, then the squaws. Below them in the twilight they could see the tiny ant-like figures on the canyon floor, picking their way across the ice covering the narrow stretches of the river and through deep drifts in the hollows. They were driving the Indians before them in a yelling, disorganized mob. From the depths of the canyon miles away, smoke was already billowing up from the villages put to the torch. A swarm of Navajos ran along the rims and the lower ledges, chanting their war songs and firing at the soldiers and rolling rocks down on them.

Kintiel grabbed Rim's arm with a force that hurt. "You've got to get to Carson. If any of my people reach you now, you'll be put to death."

Rim turned to see that Sherry had already followed them out. Pallor lay like chalk against her face as she stared into the canyon, and her hands were buried in her skirt. Kintiel saw Rim looking at her and said: "She will go too." He turned to one of his squaws. *"Da lis la nii."*

"Do tah," the woman said. *"Do tah. . . ."*

Then she turned into the cave. In a moment she reappeared with a woolen cloak for Sherry. Kintiel took Rim's elbow, turning him down the trail.

"What about you? Carson's got orders to shoot you on sight."

"I will protect you from my people," Kintiel said, "and you will protect me from yours." He smiled. "As well as you can now that my people are witnessing Kit Carson's fire dance!"

Gontzo was still toiling up the trail toward them, calling in a shrill voice. Going down, they met him. Gontzo clutched at Rim, pleading with him. "Please, *Belinkana,* tell *Ahdilohee* it isn't his coat. Just an old man's story. I had to have something. They paid so little attention to me. How could I have taken it from such a great warrior? Even in the juice of my youth. . . ."

"You stay up here," Rim told him. "They won't harm an old man."

"You do not know the *Belinkanas.*" Gontzo started to unbutton the coat, shivering in the chill. "Take it to him, take it to *Ahdilohee,* show him it is not his coat. Just an old man's lie."

Kintiel hurried them past before Gontzo could divest himself of the garment, and he followed, begging pitiably. As the trail switched back on itself, Rim looked up once at the prehistoric caves. Horse Girl had stepped onto the ledge with the squaws. She made him think of one of their goddesses; she made him think of First Woman, looking down upon him, giving him her last, sad benediction.

The towering walls seemed to tremble and reel with the deafening echoes of rifle fire. The whole canyon was swarming with figures now, as a line of blue-coated men drove a broken crowd of warriors back into the hogans of the Bead Clan. Guns made a bright, spitting flash in the twilight and black powder smoke thickened over the struggling figures. A rock came crashing down from above and Rim threw Sherry flat against the wall, pinning her there with his own body as the boulder struck the trail five feet ahead, breaking off half of the ledge in its passage and bounding on down. For a moment Sherry's soft body trembled against him, her hands gripping his arms. Then a new rattle of musketry rolled up from below, seemingly from the west.

"The troops are coming in from the gateway, too," Kintiel said. "They'll catch Standing Waters between them."

From behind they heard a new sound, husky voices singing the war chant. They looked up to see half a dozen braves passing the caves and coming down the trail after them. Kintiel grasped Rim's elbow again, rushing him on. One of the following warriors fired at them. The bullet ricocheted against the wall with an unearthly howl.

Below them was bedlam. Smoke from the hogans of the Bead Clan filled the gorge like a black pall. Descending into this, they were cut off from the sight of the Navajos following them. They got a shadowy glimpse of the burning village in the black haze of smoke. A group of Navajos seemed to be making a stand among the blazing hogans. The hollow boom of their captured Harper's Ferries joined the diabolic crackle of flames, filling the canyon with an unholy din. Rim saw blue-coated troopers breaking through here and there, dropping to one knee in the ruddy light of the flames, firing. A fire dance worthy of the *tchindis!*

A rush of howling warriors pushed their charge back. There was the deafening crash of a score of guns. A pair of the troopers pitched on their faces and four others pulled together and retreated, loading their guns and firing. A bearded sergeant appeared, his face grimed black with powder smoke.

"Rally on me, we've another squad coming, rally on me!"

Kintiel pointed at him, shouting at Rim, "Get to that officer now. You will be safe."

As Rim reached the bottom of the trail, a line of half-naked Navajos broke from the burning hogans, coughing and cursing in the smoke, opening fire on the sergeant. The man was hit and went down. His four troopers broke again, retreating back through the holocaust.

The Indians followed, firing wildly, their line spreading across the floor of the canyon and cutting Rim off from the troops in that direction. At the same time, rising over the booming echoes of gunfire and the crash of tumbling boulders, they heard the war chant.

It was the warriors who had followed down the trail. They appeared out of the smoke like hounds on a scent, bent over and trotting, chanting in their weird voices.

"We cannot wait for the soldiers to break through from the west," Kintiel called. "We must meet those coming from the east."

The braves coming off the trail forced them to cross the canyon before they could turn east, however. They ran toward the burning hogans, trying to lose themselves in the smoke. They heard the war chant fading and wavering, as the braves circled to locate them.

As they passed the fringe of the burning village, a figure stumbled toward them out of the smoke. His naked upper body was black with grime, shining with sweat. He doubled over, trying to run, hugging his belly. At first Rim thought it was a wounded man. Then he recognized Standing Waters.

The surprise of seeing the man stopped Kintiel and Rim and Sherry for an instant. Then, pulling a knife from his belt, Kintiel stepped in front of Rim. Standing Waters saw them and stopped, showing surprise as great as theirs. He no longer seemed tall or great-chested. His bent position, the drawn and gaunt look of his face made him look as dried-up and haggard as Gontzo. He stumbled forward, and Kintiel held the knife out.

A few feet from Kintiel, the headman of the Bead Clan stumbled and fell to his knees. He was still hugging his belly and wheezing like a man in great pain.

Standing Waters turned to Rim. *"Shilleh,"* he said. Rim understood that much. Then the man broke into Spanish. "Please, *Belinkana,* intercede for me. He's killing me. The bead is eating its way through my entrails. I dreamed of bear all last night. It hurts so, where he shot me with the bead."

"Don't be a fool," Rim said. "You can't believe he really shot you. . . ."

"He's killing me. I cannot stand the pain. I beg of you. The *tchindis* are in me. Tell Kintiel I will give him anything to get them out, anything!"

He fell to the ground, doubled up in agony, groveling at Kintiel's feet, whining like a baby. It was a shocking sight. At the same time, the war chant was growing louder behind them. Kintiel grabbed Rim's arm, pulling him on. They ran toward the river, leaving Standing Waters writhing and sobbing on the ground.

They crossed a cornfield full of blackened, smoldering shucks. Beyond that a pair of Indians lay sprawled on the frozen ground, motionless, and a third was crawling away, trailing a thin streak of blood. Ahead lay the stone wall of a corral.

They had almost reached it when a squad of New Mexican volunteers ran from the burning village behind them. A black-faced corporal saw Kintiel's blanket through the smoke and shouted at his men in Spanish.

"It's a *yei* blanket. Nobody but Kintiel would wear that. Fire at will!"

Rim turned toward him. "Corporal, we're Americans. Don't shoot."

But the crash of guns drowned him out. Kintiel cried out and stumbled to one knee. Unable to make himself heard above the rifle fire, Rim ran to the man. He saw blood welling from Kintiel's leg and slipped an arm about him. Together, with Sherry running ahead, they stumbled toward the rock wall. The soldiers behind were lost in the swirling mists of smoke, firing blindly. With bullets thumping into the rocks and glancing off in screaming ricochets, Rim and Kintiel threw themselves behind the wall. Then Rim got to his knees and shouted: "Cease fire, damn you, we're Americans!"

But again the deafening din of crashing musketry and the bedlam of multiplied echoes drowned him out. Kintiel lay against the rocks, holding his bloody thigh and breathing shallowly. "Get out now," he said. "Go to the soldiers coming from the east. These mean to kill me."

"I can't leave you. I've got to stop them."

"They will kill you before they know who you are."

Rim turned to Sherry. "Get across the river. Hunt for those troops coming from the gateway."

She shook her head, lips pressed tight. They could hear the calls of the corporal now, the pound of running boots. Rim tried to get Sherry on her feet.

"You'll get hit here."

"I won't leave you."

He saw the expression in her face then. All the fear was gone. All the misery and apathy and defeat of these last weeks. Her cheeks were bright and her eyes were wide and luminous. It was the same look he'd seen in the runaway wagon, when she'd refused her chance to jump.

"*Chindash!*" Kintiel swore. "Get out. Both of you."

For answer, Rim turned toward the troops again, cupping his hands around his mouth. "Corporal, for God's sake, we're Americans. Halt, cease fire, damn you!"

A gun crashed and its echoes boomed against the walls and drowned his voice in a vast pool of reverberations. A shadowy figure came running around the far end of the wall, rifle at the ready. Rim jumped up, bawling at him. But the white surface of the *yei* blanket gleamed like a light in the haze of smoke, and the man's rifle exploded.

After firing, the man clubbed his rifle

and ran down the wall. In a rage, Rim stood up to meet him, shouting. "We're white, damn you, can't you see that now?"

Coming out of the smoke, the man almost pitched on his face, trying to halt his dead run. He gaped at Rim in utter surprise. Then he turned and shouted.

"*¡Por Dios, hay blancos aqui! ¡No tiren!*"

Someone shouted in a surprised way, out in the smoke. There was more shouting and calling and then the corporal materialized out of the smoke and the dusk, followed by half a dozen dark-faced volunteers. They climbed over the wall, jabbering in Spanish, asking Rim a score of questions. Without answering, he turned back to Kintiel. The Mexican's ball had found his mark.

The medicine man lay on his back, with Sherry kneeling helplessly beside him. His hand clutched his chest and blood pumped through his fingers in a viscid, red tide. Rim went to one knee at his side. Kintiel took a shallow breath, coughing feebly. He opened his eyes to look at Rim.

"My mission is over, *Belinkana*," he

whispered. "Yours has just begun."

His eyes fluttered, turned glassy, slowly closed. All the tension went out of his great body and it slackened against the ground. Rim had never thought he could feel sentiment for this enigmatic man, yet now he had a moment of emotion as intense and poignant as that he had known upon hearing of his father's death.

At last he picked up the edge of the blanket and drew it across Kintiel until it covered his face.

Chapter Seventeen

Colonel Kit Carson had established his headquarters at the mouth of the canyon. Here, in the confines of a dusty, little tent, he greeted Rim and Sherry. Carson paced back and forth as they told him of the guns, disbelief squinting his keen eyes. He ran a lean hand through his shaggy hair, shook his head.

"It's hard to believe."

"You can't afford to doubt it."

Carson nodded, pacing again. "All right, suppose it's true. What do you suggest?"

"Give me a company of men. Let me comb the country between here and Wingate."

"I can't spare you even a squad."

"You've captured Chelly."

"I have all these prisoners to handle. The wildest of the lot, Fannin. If I weaken my force, we're liable to have a massacre here as well as at Wingate."

Rim's face turned gaunt with impatient anger. "The Army faces this right now because they wouldn't take the trouble to investigate before."

"The Army has its hands full," Carson said. "If they sent out a detail to trace down every wild rumor, they wouldn't have any men left to handle this Indian menace. My hands are tied, Fannin. My orders are to smash the Navajos. I can't spare any men to hunt out a mythical spy ring. For all I know, those guns may be at Defiance now, in the hands of the Army."

It was Rim's turn to pace savagely. "Can't you even give me a few men? We can't just sit by and. . . ."

"All right." Carson was at the end of his patience. His voice cracked like a whip. "I can give you one man. Fact is, I'll be glad to get rid of him. He got into some of that Indian *toghlepai* the first night he wandered into camp and he's been drunk ever since."

"Wandered in?"

"A man out of your wagon train. One of my patrols picked him up south of here. Sergeant Briggs."

They found him near the wall of the canyon playing freeze-out with a pair of mahogany-faced volunteers. When he saw Rim, he jumped up with a wild whoop. It was a jubilant meeting. Briggs wasn't so drunk as Carson claimed, but he still grabbed Rim in a bear hug and did a crazy jig with him.

"You old dog robber!" he shouted. "I thought that beautiful black hair was hangin' in some hogan."

"How did you get out?" Rim asked. "The last I saw you were carrying the whole attack in a one-man charge."

"That damn nag ran twenty miles with me before she dropped. I was lost in the sandstorm then. Musta wandered a week before that patrol found me. I never saw so much country without a saloon."

When he had quieted, Rim told him of their mission. Briggs was elated. "You couldn't make me happier." He spat. "Bein' with these volunteers is weakenin' my morale. They don't know a Parrot shell from a Minie ball."

Carson had promised them arms, mounts, and rations. With Sherry, they went to the cavalry bivouac. All about them now, the Indians were coming in under guard. Miserable, starved-looking, shivering in the cold, they stumbled past in a constant stream. A headman with a bloody bandage on his leg hobbled by, supported by two younger men. A pair of women herding a flock of frightened, wide-eyed children followed. Then an old hag, her head hidden in a shawl, wailing mournfully for her dead son.

Reaching the horse lines, they found that Carson's order had already gone out. Two volunteers were saddling cavalry mounts for Rim and Briggs, and a corporal had been sent to the quartermaster with a requisition for their rations. Briggs didn't like the look of one of the mounts and went over to give the volunteers the benefit of his scathing tongue.

That left Rim and Sherry alone on the edge of the bivouac, with the shadowy line of refugees from Chelly passing them at a distance. Sherry saw Rim look that way and sensed what was in his mind.

"Perhaps you should say good-bye to Horse Girl."

"It would take too long to find her," he said. "Time is precious now. She'll understand."

"She's in love with you."

It was a statement, quiet, certain,

holding no rancor, no hint of jealousy. It surprised him. He shook his head helplessly.

"I never quite knew. How could she be, Sherry? We only spoke a few words."

"Maybe you didn't have to speak at all. Who knows how it happens to a girl like that? It can come to anybody in an instant, Rim. Maybe the first look was enough."

It seemed a fitting explanation for Horse Girl, with her affinity to the deep sources of life. He no longer wondered or questioned. Yet he had become aware of the change in Sherry's tone, its quiet surety, its calm. There was none of the misery or broken defeat he had known these last weeks. He felt a hope generate in him.

"She killed a man for you," Sherry said. She took a long breath. "I suddenly feel very shallow. Very pale." She raised her eyes to him. "Very ashamed."

The hope was growing stronger now. It was hard to hold it in check. He had to be sure. "Ashamed?" he asked.

"That's the way love should be, shouldn't it? The kind of love you wanted from me, and I could never give.

A woman willing to kill for a man, if she had to."

"This is a different world out here, Sherry."

"Maybe that's what I needed." She turned to look at the walls of the canyon behind, smoky and unreal in the darkness. "The squaws took me out on the mesa yesterday, Rim. You can see so far, can't you? So much. It looked beautiful to me, Rim. For the first time in my life, it looked beautiful to me." She gazed up at him. "Maybe I've found myself out here. I can see the truth in what you told me . . . about what happened. I can't put it into words. But I'm not afraid any more."

The hope would not be checked any longer. It rose in him, poignant, choking. He knew the words she couldn't find. She had feared so many things in this land — its cruelty, its barbarism, its savagery. And now she had been subjected to it all. When the worst had happened, what was there left to fear? It had been bad; it had shocked and dazed and humiliated her. But she had come through it. She saw that she had met it, and survived it. And in surviving it, she had discovered what many others had found: the fear itself is often far worse than the thing feared.

It was an individual matter. A weaker person might have been broken on the wheel. But Rim had seen this strength in Sherry, this courage. Perhaps she was right. Perhaps this was what she had needed. A shock strong enough to jar her loose from false attitudes and spurious fears.

"Maybe we've both found ourselves, Sherry," he said.

Her face was turned up to his, like a satin cameo in the dusky light. "It seems cruel . . . to be torn apart now."

"I have to go. Carson will take you to Wingate with him. We'll meet there in a few days." He searched her face. "Are you afraid, Sherry?"

She moistened her lips; her head tilted back till her loosened hair spilled over her shoulders like a cascade of honey. "No, Rim."

It was a whisper. Her lips were parted and a tremor ran through her body. She was but inches from him and he realized what she wanted him to do, what she was asking for. He took her in his arms and he kissed her.

She met it willingly, fiercely. No holding back now, no walls between them. The passion he had only glimpsed in her before blossomed like a flame, more than a passion of the body, a passion of the spirit, coming from all the pain and shock she had learned to endure out here, coming from the knowledge of years wasted behind a veil of fear and false modesty. For a moment a great wind seemed to sweep down the canyon, roaring like a flame, booming like thunder, and he was closer to a knowledge of life than his mind alone could ever take him.

Then it was over, and Sherry pulled back a little, a deep and shuddering breath running through her body, and he saw Sergeant Briggs standing like a shadow by the horses, waiting for him.

Chapter Eighteen

When he was sober, Briggs was a good man to have along. He knew how to travel. He was a light rider and didn't beefsteak his horse and he got as much out of the animal as any Indian could, in this country. It was a cruel journey. Rim was cold all the time. His hands were numb and his face was whipped raw by a wind that never seemed to stop blowing. Having been stationed at both Defiance and Wingate, Briggs knew the route, and Rim let him lead.

Four days of it. Four days of fighting snow and sleet and ice and cold. Then Fort Wingate, in a land of crimson cliffs and broken mesas. Since early summer now conquered Navajos had been gathering here, awaiting the time when they should be sent on to Fort Sumner, sent in with detachments of troops as Carson defeated them in his westward march. Hundreds of temporary hogans of brush or wattle stood forlornly about the adobe buildings of the fort, stretching for miles in every direction.

The Indians stood or squatted in sullen groups before these miserable shelters, staring like statues at Rim and Briggs. Rim finally got talk from one of them, a headman of the Lucan Clan, named Hosteen Juanico. He could give Rim no information. The burden of his conversation had to do with complaints about their treatment. The Indians were still starving, despite the rations handed out by the military. They had been given nothing but rancid bacon and moldy flour. Used to jerked beef, the women were keeping the bacon till it spoiled, did not know how to cook with the refined flour, even lacked knowledge of how to grind the coffee berries they had been rationed. Restlessness was growing among the young braves; already riots had broken out and many of them were escaping to the desert again.

Rim could see how wretched The People were. The place was like an open powder keg. And the match to set off the explosion would be those guns.

In charge of Wingate was Major Simms. Rim reported to him with Carson's written orders. Simms admitted the Indians' complaints, but claimed their plight would be improved as soon as he had his commissary organized. He showed as much doubt of Rim's story as Carson had. There had been nothing to arouse his suspicions in camp. Had the guns arrived at Fort Defiance yet? No, Simms admitted, he had received no word of their arrival. But the storms could have delayed the trains. And he couldn't release any of his men to help Rim track down such nebulous suspicions. He had his hands full controlling the Navajos.

It was the resistance Rim had become used to. He couldn't even get angry any more. He had one hope left, one more question to ask Simms. Kintiel had named Dee Bartlett as the Confederate contact man. Rim asked the major if the squaw man was in camp. Simms told him Bartlett had opened a sutler's store just off the post.

They found the sutler's store not far from headquarters, no more than an open ramada with a thatched roof sagging under the weight of snow two days old. The bar was a pair of raw planks set on barrels, dusty troopers crowded three deep against it, and the reek of forty-rod whiskey lay as thick as syrup over it all. Rim saw Briggs's lips go slack and wet, and gave him a hard look. The sergeant wiped his nose and snorted and mumbled something about how long it had been.

Behind the bar Rim caught a glimpse of Dee Bartlett. He wore his same rotten, bearskin coat; beard stubble covered his furrowed jaw like a gray hedge. He was pouring liquor into rusty tin cups.

"I want you to watch him," Rim said. "If he asks, give him a cock-and-bull story. You think you're the only survivor of the wagon train. You got picked up by Carson's patrol and now you're attached to the command here. It's a natural story and I think he'll swallow it. Just don't tell him I'm here. If he leaves camp, trail him. If Yaki or any of his skinners contacts Bartlett, follow him."

"And you?"

"I'm going to hunt for his daughter. She might be here."

Briggs laughed heartily. "A fine couple of spies. I get drunk and you go wenching."

"You don't get and I don't go," Rim

said. "This is the only lead we've got, Briggs. You know Yaki's weakness for women. Corsica was one of his biggest weaknesses. If they're around here, they'll be getting together. Now, stand your watch and lay off the liquor."

Briggs grinned wryly, mocking Rim with a salute. "Yes, sir."

Rim left him there by the ramada and walked back through the troops coming off the post to the sutler's store, keeping out of Bartlett's sight all the time. He was sure the troopers would know if Corsica was in camp, and stopped a pair to ask them. They grinned slyly and told him the girl was with her mother's people, the Many Hogans Clan. It took Rim an hour to find them. In a dry wash, half filled with snow-drifts, were a half dozen hogans. Before them huddled a crowd of old men and squaws and half-naked children. There was enough wood for but two fires, and not enough room around these feeble blazes for all. Every few minutes the front ranks moved back, allowing another shivering group to have the privilege of dubious warmth.

As Rim approached, he saw one of the women detach herself from the group and move toward him, slowly at first, then faster, an eager smile breaking her face. It was Corsica, as exotic, as vivid as ever. Yet, somehow, he did not feel the old rush of excitement.

"Reem, Reem! I theenk you dead. From where you come? What happen?"

She was in his arms, face upturned eagerly, cheeks shining, eyes dancing with the old mischief. But he made no move to kiss her and she felt the ungiving withdrawal of his body. She stepped back, frowning, hurt.

"Corsica," he said. He felt helpless. "I'm sorry."

A pixy light came into her eyes. "Another woman, maybe?"

"Sherry."

She looked surprised. "That empty jar?"

"She's changed, Corsica. We both found something out there."

She smiled wryly. "So it is. No look like it hurt so much. You and me, we have fun for a while. Is enough. Laugh. Say *adios*."

He could not help smiling. "In a way, there was never one like you, Corsica."

"Thank you, Reem."

"Are you here for long?"

Some of her cynical humor left her. "They say all Navajos go on long walk to *Hwalle*. Me they would not let stay in Tucson no longer. My father, he breeng. Back to my mother's people."

"Perhaps you'll be happier here."

She looked up at him, a darkness of complete misery in her eyes. "How? Do they want me?" Her voice grew bitter. "No more than my father he want me."

For a moment he knew a deep pity for this girl lost between two peoples. "If there's something I could do . . . more food, better quarters."

She lowered her head again, her silence telling him what a futile gesture such an offer was. He spoke again, awkwardly.

"I understand some of the wagon train got through. Was Yaki with them?"

She raised her head, then smiled almost tauntingly. "Yes."

"I should be jealous."

She rose to his bantering. "You should."

"Was he the one who told you I was dead?"

She nodded.

"Natural he should think so," Rim said. "We got cut off. Lost in that sandstorm. He still owes me wages for the part of the trip I made. Can I find him around here?"

She shook her head. "His camp I no know. He say he come back."

"When?"

"Tonight."

Rim thought fast, then shook his head. "Too late. I'm leaving in an hour. Tell him to see me in Tucson."

He hesitated, not knowing how to say good-bye. She had recovered her mischievous spirits now. Her laugh was indulgent.

"I have say good-bye to many men, Reem. Is no reason to feel bad."

He answered her smile. She held out her hand and he took it. "Good-bye, Corsica. I'll see you again."

"*Adios,* my frien'."

His first impulse was to get Briggs and tell him what was happening. But the sergeant was fifteen minutes off, on the other side of the sprawling Indian encampment. And Yaki might come while Rim was gone. So he circled out to a sandstone ridge overlooking the site of the Many Hogans camp. Here, screened by scrub oak and piñon, he took up his vigil. Dusk thickened into night; the fires became brighter against the velvety darkness. Then a young brave galloped into the Many Hogans camp, the ruddy blaze flickering up across the coppery shine of his naked, sweating torso. Even from the distance of the ridge, Rim could hear his voice, rising and falling in what sounded almost like one of their chants.

Soon a strange moaning began to emanate from the squaws. It gathered volume, spreading away from Rim to the camp sites of farther clans, until the whole desert seemed to be wailing. And Rim knew what it meant. The first batch of prisoners must have arrived from Canyon de Chelly. This was the Navajos' first knowledge that their hereditary stronghold had fallen.

Rim's temples began to pound with a stirring excitement. Kintiel had thought that Yaki was awaiting this — holding those captured guns till the wild clans of Canyon de Chelly added their numbers to the warriors already here, making the certainty of a massacre more complete. If that was true, this was the night.

Risking detection, Rim led his horse down the ridge, closer to camp. The young Indian who had brought the news rode off, and the squaws gathered around their fires, wailing and chanting, shawls hiding their heads. One of the old men began an oration, jerking his skinny arms back and forth to emphasize his words.

It was a barbaric scene, with the wailing of hundreds of women rising from the depths of the night, and the old man's husky chanting going on and on. And into this rode another man. The dogs began yapping before Rim could see him. But Rim drew even closer, with but a fringe of mesquite between him and camp, for the animals would not make such a fuss unless it was a stranger. Fire light licked up the rider as he entered its flickering circle, illuminating the gigantic, rawboned figure of Yaki Peters.

He kicked his dun saddler through the yapping dogs and circling children, looking from right to left till he saw Corsica. Then he stopped his mount, slouching in the saddle, hemp-slack, mule-gaunt. The light made a greasy shine against the ridges of his cheekbones, left black pits of shadow in the bony hollows of his face. His words were clearly audible to Rim.

"What the hell's fixin'?" he asked.

Corsica stopped by his mule. "Canyon de Chelly has been taken. The first prisoners have arrived."

Yaki sat up so sharply in the saddle that his mule twitched. Then he wheeled the animal and kicked it into a gallop out of camp. Corsica took a couple of running steps behind him, completely surprised.

"Yaki!" she called. Then she stopped, frowning after him.

Rim was already in the saddle, running his animal right out into the pack of snapping dogs, scattering them. Corsica wheeled at the sound of running hoofs. He drew the horse in hard, a foot away from her. With the excited animal rearing and pirouctting beneath him, he called sharply:

"Corsica, get to Sergeant Briggs. He's at your dad's store. Tell him I've found Yaki Peters. We're heading south."

She looked at him blankly. "Reem, what you do?"

"I haven't time to explain. Just do this for me. If you have any faith in me at all, do it!"

She shook her head helplessly. "Very

well. For you. But I no see how that *borrachon* can help you. The headman he just came back from the store. He say Briggs is blind drunk. Cause big trouble."

Rim fought to hold his horse, staring at Corsica with a helpless fury running through him. Damn you, Briggs. But anger was no help now. Yaki Peters was almost out of sight, a dim, shadowy shape appearing briefly as he ran his mule past the last fire on the edge of the Indian encampment. Rim spurred his horse into a run out of the Many Hogans camp.

He knew there was a guard — sentries placed every few hundred yards and mounted patrols that scouted the borders of the camp regularly. But Yaki must have known the holes to slip through. He made a sudden right-angle turn past a hogan on the fringe of camp and ran into the darkness. Rim spurred his horse to catch up, knowing that if he were too far behind he would run into the patrol Yaki had calculated to miss.

He left the light of the last fire behind and plunged into blackness after Yaki. He heard a shout at his right.

"Halt! Who goes there?" There was a shot and a Minie ball whipped past him and then the same voice began bawling: "Corporal o' the guard, corporal o' the guard!"

Then that was behind him. The sentries had heard two horses go by in the night. They would probably think it was a pair of braves, willing to risk starvation and death in the winter desert rather than face the confinement and humiliation of the long walk. This was a common occurrence and Major Simms couldn't spare any men for pursuit every time it happened.

So Rim was alone now, following Yaki.

From high ground he saw the rider making a barely visible moving stain on the desert again. Using the cover of saguaro and mesquite, Rim followed till they struck mountains studded with piñon and scrub oak. The moon was up now and he could see Yaki's tracks in the sandy loam. A trail Briggs could have followed if he had been sober.

Beyond the hills they came to a broad flat, covered inches deep with black cinders, and Rim knew where they were heading, now. The malpais, the lava country. It was a natural place to hold the wagons, a tortured, cruel land, avoided by white and Indian alike, where a man could stay a lifetime with practically no chance of discovery.

The horse sank fetlock deep in the cinders, snorting, whinnying, fighting for every step he took. But Yaki's mule was doing the same far ahead, its sounds covering whatever noise Rim's animal made. There were jagged uplifts of lava, shining evilly in the moonlight. Following these, Rim could remain unseen and yet keep up with Yaki.

Rim did not know how far they traveled before they reached the real lava beds. It must have been the better part of the night. Finally, with the moon waning, he mounted a ridge and beheld a fantastic sight. On every side, stretching for uncounted miles to a dim horizon, were gigantic waves, black as jet, glistening like wet ink, dipping and rolling and cresting in a thousand, incredible, volcanic gyrations. Rim could hear Yaki's mule clattering across the hard surface far ahead. He followed and finally saw where the man had dropped off into a gully that ran a tortured course through the weird phantasmagoria of nature. Here were the wagon tracks, dug deeply in the baked earth. Rim felt a grudging admiration for Yaki. Few men could have got those ponderous, fully loaded Murphys this far in such a land.

All about him rolled the grotesque black lava now, gigantic waves, breaking against the beach of time for a million years. Then the moon was gone and he was traveling in pre-dawn blackness. He lost track of Yaki ahead. All he could do was follow the wash, dismounting to feel for the tracks in the baked clay of its bottom.

At last, from far ahead, he saw a rosy glow silhouetting the twisted ridges of lava. The light of a campfire. And then Yaki's braying shout.

"Roll out, you skinners, roll out! We're breakin' camp before sunup."

Rim dismounted, ground-hitching his weary horse, and moved cautiously forward on foot. With a hand numbed by the winter chill, he fumbled the gun Carson had given him from its holster. Rounding a tongue of lava, he came suddenly upon the scene.

The whole train of wagons was corralled in a circle on a vast cinder flat,

the flickering blaze of campfires silhouetting the hooped tops and high beds.
He was so close that the nearest outfit
was but a few feet away, a bull whip
slung on its brake arm. Already the
circle of wagons was echoing to the
curses and grumbling of skinners as
they rolled from their blankets, the
braying of mules, the gun-shot snap of
whips. The cinder dust began to boil up
beneath stamping hoofs till it hung like
a black pall in the air, almost blotting
out the ruddy light of the fires.

Rim crouched there a moment, looking beneath the bed of the wagon, un-
decided. He had no hope of stopping
them alone. It was no time for foolish
heroics. Yaki must have established
some meeting place where the weapons
could be transferred to Indians who
could get them back into camp a few at
a time without arousing suspicion. And
if Rim left now and tried to get the
military, he might not be able to find
the train again before the guns were
distributed.

He had not moved when it happened.
A figure suddenly materialized from the
black haze of cinder ash, backing a pair
of balky mules into the tongue of the

wagon next to the one behind which Rim crouched. Automatically Rim started to back toward the ledge of lava behind him. Then he stopped himself, realizing how the action would expose him.

But the movement had given him away. The man let go of his mules and started walking toward the corner of the Murphy. "Haskell, that you?"

He broke off, stopping abruptly, near enough to recognize Rim in the dim light of the fires. The two of them stood twenty feet apart, facing each other. Yaki Peters and Rim Fannin.

Rim could see the utter astonishment in Yaki's face. The man had his whip in his hand, its long lash dragging on the ground behind him. He stared emptily at Rim, his mouth gaping open, but hazel eyes wide with shock. Rim had his gun pointed at the man now, and it was cocked.

"Yaki," he said, "make a sound and I'll kill you."

Yaki let his air out in a long, sighing sound. "Wal, if that don't take the curl out'n the pig's tail."

"I know what it's about now," Rim said. "I know it's Confederate and I know how big it is. Are you the boss?"

Yaki had recovered his composure. He grinned lazily, maliciously. "You'll never find out who's runnin' this show."

There was a sudden new bedlam of hee-hawing mules. Squealing and braying, they smashed into the other side of the wagon. The whole outfit jerked and shuddered. The din startled Rim, and he could not help looking that way. He tried to turn back, realizing his mistake. But he was too late.

Yaki was already throwing himself behind the corner of the wagon, jerking his whipstock over his shoulder. Rim fired at the man's shadowy figure. But Yaki's upper body was already blocked off by the wagon bed and Rim's bullet did no more than chew off wood where the man's head had been a moment before. Rim's frozen thumb hooked over the Patterson's hammer. Before he could cock it, thirty feet of snarling lash came out of nowhere and cracked his arm so violently he thought it was broken.

The blow knocked him stumbling against the front wheel of the wagon. Yaki lunged from the protection of the bed, jerking his whipstock once more over his knobby shoulder.

Rim knew he had only that next instant to act. His gun had been knocked from his hand and lay twenty feet away. He could never reach it in time. But the other mule whip was coiled around the brake arm, above his head.

He couldn't get the whip and escape Yaki's lash too. With a grunt, he lunged for the whip, throwing his left arm across his face.

"That's hit, coon. Le's fry some back fat!"

The lash came hissing out of mid-air and struck Rim's arm with shocking force. Again he thought it was broken, and could not help crying out. But it had protected his face. Only the bull-horn popper got through, digging a bloody furrow in his forehead.

And he had his whip.

Stumbling away from the wagon, half blinded by the blood in his eyes, Rim saw Yaki drag his blacksnake back for another lash. Rim stopped himself with feet spread wide to keep from falling, shaking his lash out with a quick flirt. For that instant suspended in time they faced each other, and the fitness of this struck Rim. It was as if the moment had been woven into the inevitable pattern of fate, and nothing they could have done would have ended it differently. Remembering Sean Fannin, whipped to death on the Santa Cruz, remembering the one-armed rebel lying under a heap of rocks on the same river, Rim accepted this with a savage eagerness.

"If you're thinkin' about Steve Swan," Yaki told him, "you want to remember what happened to him."

"I've been remembering every night and every day since it did happen." Something thin and bitter had flattened Rim's tone out.

"Yeah, go ahead," called Yaki, holding his whipstock up in his right hand, and reaching out with his left to curl those two helpless fingers in about the hickory handle. "It looks like the Pike County coon is goin' to play muleskinner."

His hand swept back over his shoulder. It was the same opening he had given Steve Swan. Rim refused to take it, allowing his own lash to remain flat on the ground, waiting. Yaki saw that his feint had failed, and let his whip go back in a genuine over-the-shoulder, cracking twenty-four feet behind him. Then he dragged it forward again, with all the lash that could possibly be put into the deadly snake. Rim waited till it seemed right in his face. Then he lifted his lash straight off the ground to foul the oncoming popper.

Yaki divined Rim's intent and, in that last instant, dragged back on his three foot whipstock, his popper cracking mid-air, a foot from Rim's face. Rim's own lash made a futile hiss between himself and the end of Yaki's whip, and began to drop back.

Yaki swept his whip handle in a wide, vicious, jerking motion from right to left, to keep the end of his blacksnake in mid-air till Rim's whip had dropped below fouling range. Rim dragged his own whipstock across in front of his body the way Lonesome had taught him, to keep his own snake in mid-air. When Yaki saw that Rim's whip would not fall back, he swept his stock back the other way, from left to right. It became a duel now, each of them sweeping his whip back and forth to keep it aloft, each seeking to foul the other's lash, each seeking to keep his own from being fouled. Rim finally caught Yaki's, entangling their lashes, pulling him down. But he could not get his lash into the air quick enough after they were ensnared, and the duel started again. Back and forth, side to side, up and down, until Rim thought his arm would drop off. He was dripping sweat, blinded by it, gasping with the terrible effort of endurance. He realized now why Lonesome had been so insistent on practicing this. The crowd which had gathered around was watching spellbound at the bizarre battle.

Finally Rim could keep it up no longer, and his arm dropped, and his whip dropped. Yaki jumped in tigerish triumph on the opening. His whip, still in mid-air, made a great, hissing arc and the popper exploded deafeningly in Rim's face.

Rim's back struck the ground with pain making bright flashes in his vision. In his effort to rise, he was struggling against the cushiony, insistent pressure of a giant feather bed.

"Hog-up, hog-up, straw bed and no cover, corn bread and no butter, bra-a-ah!"

With Yaki's raucous bellow in his ears, Rim heard the snarl of the whip again. Agony stamped his ribs. His whole being. He was knocked back into the crowd. For a moment, their fetid press held him. Then they had pulled away from him. He rolled over, blood draining into his eyes. What was it Lonesome had said? Only one way to get Yaki. Get in under that whip. Rim had tried it that first time, when Yaki had killed Steve. Only he had no whip then. He had one now. The only way. The only way.

Yaki lifted his mule whip off the ground in front of him and snapped the whole length out without using back-lash. It cracked Rim's knees together and wound about them, tripping him. He fell heavily on his face.

"Bra-a-ah, Pike's showing some fight now; let's fry some more hide, maw. I jes' love the smell of burnin' mule meat!"

The cinder dust hung over the flats like a black pall and Rim was choking and coughing in it as he rose to his feet and fought to keep his whip in the air. Drenched with sweat, groaning with the terrible effort of endurance, he lost track of how many times they disen-gaged, always fighting to keep their lashes in the air.

Finally, when he did not think he could last a moment longer, Rim saw Yaki's arm drop. He brought his own stock across his body in a last triumphant motion. He saw the popper sing through the air toward Yaki's face. The wagon boss tried to lift his whip off the ground again, but exhaustion had robbed him of strength. His whip was not high enough to foul Rim's lash. The whip struck Yaki, the popper whining round and round his neck.

Yaki staggered under the impact. Rim heaved, trying to spill him. But Yaki grabbed the whip, while it was still around his neck. Holding it, he brought his own lash back over his shoulder.

Rim knew if he let go of his own whip he was finished. He gave a last desperate heave, trying to free it. But Yaki's grip was like a vise. And then Yaki's whip boomed like a gun and sang back over his shoulder at Rim with all the lash it could possibly get.

It was the explosion of a Parrot shell right in Rim's face. The world went to pieces and he was falling, falling, with only one thought left to him: hang onto the whip, hang onto the whip.

"Haw, you Yankee bastard! I'm agoin'

to make a bull-tongue plow outa' you, hah! I'm agoin' to furrow the ground with your snout, hah!"

There was the detonation. There was the blinding pain across Rim's back, flopping him over, driving his face into the ground.

The snarl of the whip again. Agony stamping his ribs. His body flopping over again. But he still had his whip and it had pulled free. He was on his face now and he put his hands against the ground, pushing upward. The whip cracked across his back, driving him to the ground like a thousand pounds.

With the world spinning, Rim tried to gain his hands and knees, but the lash was coming at him again, head-high.

"You got to git his legs, son. It's the only way."

Lonesome's words were coming to him from out of the past like a whisper in his mind. Rim threw himself flat on the ground, eating dirt. Yaki's lash whined impotently above him, reaching the end of its length with a deafening crack.

Rim saw the surprise on Yaki's face. At the same time, sprawled flat, Rim swung his own stock out in a wide arc from hip to head, horizontal with the ground. Yaki tried to dance away. But Rim's lash tangled in his legs and spilled him.

Rim stumbled to his feet, pawing blood and sweat from his eyes. He swept his whipstock back. Yaki rolled over and tried to come up. His motion brought him directly into Rim's lash, as it sank back. Rim saw the lash crack against Yaki's neck, saw Yaki's head snapped to one side with violent force.

Like a rag doll doing a macabre dance, Yaki folded up. His gaunt body sprawled to the ground, looking loose and disjointed in death, with the broken neck twisted back on itself at an impossible angle.

Rim swayed on his feet, staring at the man, unable to believe it was over. A dizziness of pain and exhaustion swept through him. For a moment he thought he would fall. He stumbled to the wagon and leaned against it. For the first time he saw the man.

No telling when he had come around the tail of the wagon. No telling how long he had been standing there. It was Steve Swan.

Rim was too numb to react. He leaned

heavily against the wagon, his useless left arm hanging without feeling at his side, staring blankly at Swan. The one-armed Johnny Reb held a big Walker Colt casually in his hand, pointed at Rim's belly. But he was grinning.

"Lucky time t' come after muh whip."

Rim glanced down at the whip in his hand, eyes following its lash to the end, tipped with a popper made from a Union belt buckle. The irony of it crept dully against him.

"Don't look so shocked, Rim," Swan said. "I jes' wasn't dead down on the Santa Cruz, that's all. While Denvers was havin' his hearin', four of the skinners carried me off into the bottoms. Then they piled a heap o' stones up to look like they'd buried me."

Rim shook his head, trying to grasp the reality, the full implication of this. Finally he said, "You're the brains, then?"

Swan nodded. "Commissioned by Jeff Davis hisself. We didn't think Sherod Hunter could hold Arizona. I was supposed to git captured if he had to leave." He looked down at his empty sleeve. "Didn't figger on losin' this at Picacho pass." Then he grinned. "Purty good bargain, at that. One arm for all the gold in Arizona."

"You'll never get it."

"Neither will you. That's my job, Rim. If Jeff Davis can't have it, neither can the federal treasury."

Rim drew a shuddering breath, trying to steady himself. "You were responsible for the sand in the flour sacks."

"We thought it might put the Pimas on the warpath." Swan said. "We sent the real flour to the Confederates in Texas."

"Those twenty wagons Archuleta saw heading south?"

Swan nodded. "That's right. Only your talk musta got under Wylie Landor's hide. He went huntin' fer 'em. Found 'em camped south o' Buchanan. The teamsters caught him sneakin' up on the corral. They'd been talkin' about me. Didn't know how much he'd heard. Couldn't let him git back alive."

"But why disappear?" Rim asked.

"Before he died, Wylie claimed there was somebody with him. Now I know it was a bluff. At the time there was no way of telling. If the man with Wylie'd got the word to Carson about me, my use here was done. We hadn't planned on Yaki whuppin' me almost to death, but it came natural. Nobody'd be lookin' for a dead man to head a spy ring, would they?"

The simplicity of it angered Rim. How could he have been so blind? "And Romaine?" he asked.

"A goat, a pawn. We let him stay in business so we could use him. He still don't know how the sand got in the flour bags."

"And me?" Rim asked. "Why didn't you just let those two men finish the job that time in the Tucson alley?"

"I didn't know what was goin' on. Romaine musta done that on his own. Got tired o' you puttin' the finger on him and sent a couple of his boys around."

As Swan spoke, the Walker Colt rose till its muzzle was directed at Rim's chest. Rim's reactions were numbed by exhaustion. He was filled with a last crazy impulse to rush the man, but he knew how useless that would be. He wasn't even close enough to a wagon to try Yaki's trick. Swan cocked the gun.

"I really hate to do this, Rim. But it looks like we're about ready to go."

The gunshot jarred Rim's head. But

there was no pain. Only Swan's mouth, opening in surprise, and Swan's body going slack and crumpling to the ground.

With the sweat clammy on his forehead, Rim turned around. Sergeant Patrick Briggs lay sprawled on his belly atop the ledge of lava twenty feet behind Rim. In his hand was a Springfield, smoke issuing in a curling tendril from its barrel.

"That half-breed gal told me," he said. "Damn hard, trailin' when you're drunk."

Rim glanced over his shoulder at the pall of black ash obscuring the mêlée of braying mules and the gathered skinners. "I never thought you could do it, Briggs. Now you've got to get back. Tell Carson. . . ."

"Whole troop o' cavalry," Briggs said. "Be here in a minute."

"How did you do it? They didn't follow me."

Briggs spat. "You didn't sock Major Simms."

Rim and Briggs got back in the afternoon of the next day. Major Simms's office was full of men — Colonel Carson and his grimy, exhausted officers. The major came out of his chair like a jack-in-the-box when he saw Briggs.

"Before you turn out the firing squad," Rim said, "maybe you better hear why Briggs did it."

Carson and Simms kept shaking their heads as Rim unfolded the story. With Yaki and Swan dead, the heart had gone out of the skinners. They hadn't even put up a fight against the troop of cavalry following Briggs. About all that was left was to bring in the wagons and order Dee Bartlett's arrest.

Carson's frosty eyes twinkled. "If you were still in the Army, Fannin, I guess they'd give you a brevet or something. Maybe you'll get a reward anyway. Sherry Landor came with me."

Sergeant Briggs laughcd heartily at Rim. "I'll be damned if you weren't wrong after all. I am gittin' drunk. And . . . you're goin' wenchin'."

Rim turned and went out in long, eager strides. His arm was in a sling made from Briggs's kerchief and he still didn't know if it was broken. His eyes burned and he was weak with exhaustion and he ached all over. But none of it mattered the instant he saw her. They must have told her of his arrival. She was half running across the parade ground, her eyes shining and her hands held out to him. He met her and pulled her to him and they stood together, neither saying anything, for it was somehow beyond words.

Behind her, he could see the sun sinking into a shimmering mist on the horizon. A good omen, Horse Girl had said. *Johano-ai,* riding his turquoise horse, was scattering his sacred pollen like a golden haze at the edge of the world.

Les Savage, Jr. was an extremely gifted writer who was born in Alhambra, California, but grew up in Los Angeles. His first published story was "Bullets and Bullwhips" accepted by the prestigious Street and Smith's *Western Story Magazine*. Almost ninety more magazine stories all set on the American frontier followed, many of them published in Fiction House magazines such as *Frontier Stories* and *Lariat Story Magazine* where Savage became a superstar with his name on many covers. His first novel, *TREASURE OF THE BRASADA*, appeared in 1947, the first of twenty-four published novels to appear in the next decade. Due to his preference for historical accuracy, Savage often ran into problems with book editors in the 1950s who were concerned about marriages between his protagonists and women of different races — a commonplace on the real frontier but not in much Western fiction in that decade.

Savage died young, at thirty-five, from complications arising out of hereditary diabetes and elevated cholesterol. Noteworthy titles of his like *SILVER STREET WOMAN, OUTLAW THICKETS, RE-*

TURN TO WARBOW, *THE TRAIL*, and *BEYOND WIND RIVER* have become classics of Western fiction. *RETURN TO WARBOW* is one of four of his novels so far to have appeared as a major motion picture.

As a result of the censorship imposed on many of his works, only now have they been fully restored by returning to the author's original manuscripts. *TABLE ROCK*, Savage's last book, was even suppressed by his agent in part because of its depiction of Chinese on the frontier. It has now been published as he wrote it by Walker and Company in the United States and Robert Hale, Ltd., in the United Kingdom. Much as Stephen Crane before him, while he wrote the shadow of his imminent death grew longer and longer across his young life and he knew that, if he was going to do it at all, he would have to do it quickly. He did it well, better than almost anyone who wrote Western and frontier fiction, ever. Now that his novels and stories are being restored to what he had intended them to be, his achievement irradiated by his powerful and profoundly sensitive imagination will be with us always, as he had wanted it to be, as he had so rushed against time and mortality that it might be.

We hope you have enjoyed this Large Print book. Other Thorndike Press or Chivers Press Large Print books are available at your library or directly from the publishers.

For more information about current and upcoming titles, please call or write, without obligation, to:

Thorndike Press
P.O. Box 159
Thorndike, Maine 04986
USA
Tel. (800) 223-2336

OR

Chivers Press Limited
Windsor Bridge Road
Bath BA2 3AX
England
Tel. (0225) 335336

All our Large Print titles are designed for easy reading, and all our books are made to last.